TIME WINDOW

Searching for the Answer
To Save The Human Race

LOUIS DAIGLE

PUBLISHER'S INFORMATION

Author contact: ridaig@cox.net

ISBN   978-1-938517-57-0

© 2016 by Louis Daigle

Additionally, this is work of science fiction. License has been taken with scientific fact. The reader is advised to do his or her own research on topics of interest spurred by this novel.

ACKNOWLEDGMENTS

I could have not completed that book without the encouragement and support of the following people. Thank you all.

Author Richard Parker. Thank you Richard for your continued support editing and improving my book. Carl Beckman, deceased, former University of Rhode Island professor for his support and urging to finish my book. Ken Reynolds, retired engineer whose enthusiasm for the manuscript kept him urging me to get it into print. Caitlin Taves, Brightview Senior Vibrant Living Assistant, for her patience helping me tame my unruly new laptop.

DEDICATION

To my wife and life partner, Terry, and my children
Susan, Jo Ann, Peter and Jeffery

CONTENTS

PROLOGUE

Nature's universal events calendar has just turned to a new page. As the next phase of the creation cycle evolves, humankind on planet Earth is caught completely off guard, without a clue as to what is underway.

Humanity will misread Nature's emerging, subtle signals and may come close to self-destruction. Crises of enormous proportions will threaten man's very existence on the planet. Will it be possible to discover meaningful answers to this dire dilemma in time?

A world-wide scientific community will mount a desperate program to comprehend what is actually happening and try to extend humans' lease on Earth.

The story that follows is fiction and but a tiny window in time during which humanity finally realizes that its tenure on this planet is totally under NATURE's control. We must await our fate.

The time frame is the not-too-distant future. Read on.

1

The time was 1:15AM, January 13th, and traffic on Interstate 84 to Danbury from Hartford, Connecticut, was light. Ice slicks on the highway made driving extremely risky, but one car was headed west to Danbury in spite of the wintry road hazards. Little did the driver realize that his life's destination would be altered within a very short time. Getting home to his family, after a three-day insurance seminar, was foremost on his mind.

Suddenly, a tractor-trailer came barreling across the highway divider. BAM! No time to react before the collision took place, the impact spun the car around clockwise and rammed it broadside against the trailer. Needless to say, the driver was critically injured.

"Help! Please, if anyone can hear me! Get an ambulance here right away!" the truck driver repeatedly shrieked on his CB radio. At least he had the presence of mind to call for assistance.

"Where are you? What happened? I'll relay your call to the Waterbury Police." Someone had picked up the SOS and help would arrive shortly.

"I'm about two miles west of Waterbury on Rt. 84. I just hit a car head on. We need some help—hurry!"

It took no more than five minutes before police cruisers and an ambulance arrived, lights flashing and sirens full blast. The car, completely demolished, lay on its side, one headlight eerily shining. A hospital attendant, aided by a state trooper, pried open the door on the driver's side; there was little hope of anyone surviving the brutal accident. Finally, the door was lifted enough for the attendant to work his way inside.

"Only one body; pretty bad mess. Pass me the stethoscope," the attendant called out. "His heart's still beating— get me an oxygen bottle, and let's get him out of here!"

After carefully maneuvering the hopelessly injured body out of the wrecked automobile, onto a stretcher, and into the ambulance, vital signs were still present. The truck driver was badly shaken, but not physically hurt. There were no other casualties. The ambulance headed for Waterbury General Hospital with a police escort.

The poor accident victim didn't make it, in spite of his speedy rescue. His heart stopped beating in the ER just as the attending doctor was making his preliminary examination to determine the scope of the injuries. Cause of death was internal hemorrhaging with extensive vital organ damage. As the next of kin were notified of the tragedy and his personal effects gathered, it was standard procedure to examine the deceased's wallet.

"Doctor, this man has a donor card," the nurse's aide called out.

The victim's final wish to donate vital organs prompted the doctor to immediately call for the resident surgeon to survey the remains. The process that followed was one of carefully dissecting the human cadaver in search of usable parts. In the end, the lone organ that qualified as reusable was his heart. This did not come as a surprise as it was pumping steadily right up until the end.

The next step was to wrap the heart in a protective bag with saline solution specifically designed for that purpose. It was packed in ice and placed in a thermos container for shipment. First, however, the heart was rushed to the pathology lab for tests.

The expedited identification and location of a suitable recipient for this organ would depend upon a carefully executed procedure. The auto accident victim had been pronounced dead at 1:34AM. At 2:11AM, the first microphotographs and characterization data were transmitted to the synchronous communication satellite 22,000 miles out in space and relayed back via television transmission to the Houston Medical Center in Texas and the Stanford Research Hospital in Palo Alto, California. The two were next alerted to be on the lookout for the vital information. They would search through their candidate patients for compatibility, as well as those of other medical centers in the country who performed organ transplant surgery.

At 2:47 AM the following response came out of Houston:

WE HAVE A MATCH—PLEASE SHIP VIA FASTEST CARRIER—WE ARE SCHEDULING TRANSPLANT OPERATION TO START 8:00AM.

Once the thermos container was flown to Kennedy International Airport by helicopter and placed on Delta Flight 348 nonstop to Houston, the burden of responsibility shifted to the heart transplant team of Dr. Robert Armstrong, Chief of Heart Surgery.

The hospital switchboard was busy as calls were placed to round up team members, and most importantly, Ben Davidson. He was one out of a thousand or so candidates who provided the closest match in this highly selective process. Heart transplant operations during the past ten years had become routine. The process of matching donor organs to waiting recipients was precise and scientific. There was no doubt that the selection process, improved surgical techniques, and development of antirejection drugs, all played critical roles in the phenomenally high success rate.

The Davidson family had been in a state of anticipation ever since Ben had returned home from the medical center six weeks ago. His two-month stay for treatment of a deteriorating heart condition with no hope of a cure had convinced him and his wife Mary that their options had shrunk down to one and only one—a heart transplant as soon as possible. They had been advised that a call from the Center could come at any time and to be prepared to make the short trip from their home in Galveston to the hospital, in the middle of the night if necessary.

When the telephone rang at 2:55 AM, Mary was awakened from a deep sleep, and she knew instinctively who it was. The ambulance would be at their home at 3:55 AM to transport Ben, bedridden since discharged from his last visit, back to the hospital for this life-saving corrective surgery.

Once at the hospital, Ben was immediately wheeled away by an attendant to be prepped for the operation. Mary was advised to wait at home. There would be numerous tests performed on Ben by various hospital departments; she could visit later around 6:00.

At 5:45 AM, Mary was informed of Ben's room number; she anxiously headed to him. *Please, God,* she silently prayed, *let this be the right decision, and let all go well with the operation.* When she got to his room, she felt overcome with emotion. No, I promised myself I wouldn't break down. Ben needs all the moral support I can give him.

"Hi Hon, how's my one and only doing this morning?" she said, kissing him tenderly.

Ben, quite heavily sedated, still had his wits about him and was determined to pull through the ordeal. "Hi Babe, give me six hours and I'll be a new man."

"I'm glad you feel so confident since it's your first surgery," Mary said.

"I know it's a big one, nothing compared to when you had surgery as a kid, but don't worry about me. I'm in the best of hands, and I'll make it through with flying colors."

Mary looked searchingly into his eyes. *Definitely not the time to remind him that my surgery had complications. I'm not going to mess with his positive attitude.*

They were good together and could re-enforce each other during tough moments. While reminiscing about their happy lives during the past nineteen years, Dr. Robert Armstrong appeared on the scene.

"Look who's here—my favorite couple." He greeted them with his usual friendly manner and proceeded to inspect test results that hung on a clipboard at the foot of the bed.

"All of your tests have been excellent, Ben, and we have great expectations for you. I just want to make sure that the two of you are still convinced this will be the solution to our problem. If I did not think you were making the right move, I would not hesitate to tell you, but I personally feel that the odds are good in your particular case."

"Doc, Mary and I have a lot of confidence in you. If we were able to get this far, we can chance it to go the rest of the way," Ben said as he held Mary's hand. It was obvious they were optimistic.

"Good for you, Ben, hang on to your positive attitude. I'll leave you two alone while I tend to a few details, and I'll be seeing you soon. Bye, Mary, and keep your spirits up!"

Dr. Armstrong was anxious to find out if the replacement heart had arrived yet. At the nurses' desk down the hall, he reached for the phone and dialed for news about Delta Flight 348. He let out a sigh of relief when informed the flight had just arrived, and the hospital courier was at the airport picking up the canister.

The Armstrong heart transplant team had achieved many successes during the past twenty-three years. Numerous experimental trials resulted in techniques that had paid off. During the early years, patients surviving beyond three to four years were few and far between. As time went on, the percentage of survivors steadily increased, and the life expectancy after transplant surgery also increased. The ultimate success of permanent acceptance by the body of a foreign heart without the use of antirejection drugs had not been achieved as yet, but progress was being made.

Heart transplant surgery, since the first such operation by Dr. Christian Bernhard of South Africa, had been an evolving branch of medicine which necessarily made humans the test subjects. In practically all cases, recipients were chosen for operations as a last resort when any other form of treatment was deemed hopeless. Such was still the unwritten rule, and cases like Ben Davidson were chosen on the basis of poor odds for living, without surgery, as well as a physical makeup that was more tolerant of a foreign object. Transplants of many other vital organs were performed routinely using the same rules for selection.

The operation started promptly at 8:00 AM and the freshly scrubbed team of Dr. Robert Armstrong went to work. Doctors and nurses performed like clockwork as a result of many similar operations. Total elapsed time from application of anesthetic to stapling into place the final suture (closing the chest cavity) was four hours and ten minutes. How well Ben would adapt to his new heart remained to be seen.

2

L ouis Keck and his wife, Katy, had just returned from eating dinner at their favorite "Surf and Turf" restaurant in Austin, TX. Eating out was a weekly ritual they relished. Times like these were precious as each felt contentment now that their four children were grown and pursuing their own careers as well as raising their own families. All were happily married and so far had produced a combined total of six children which made the grandparents very proud.

"Isn't it great being out here in Texas doing our own thing?" Lou said. "Now that most of our responsibilities are behind us, we can pretty much pick what we enjoy the most."

"You're such a sentimentalist. No wonder you came back to Texas," Katy replied. "To revisit your joyful youth."

After Lou parked the car in the garage, the two walked to the rear of the house and stood on the sun deck, admiring the glow of the city lights in the distance. Seeing it from the hills on the outskirts was picture perfect.

The cool night air prompted Katy to snuggle up to Lou. "Do you mind terribly if we go indoors, Hon? It's getting a bit chilly out here."

"Go on inside if you like, Dear. I'll stay out here a bit longer to enjoy the scenery, ok?" He kissed Katy, fully intending to rejoin her in a few minutes.

Lou gazed at the Texas sky. It was a cool January night, and he was awed at the number of stars he could see with his naked eye. Ever since moving to Austin last year to accept a staff position at the Institute's fusion laboratory, he had gotten into the habit of studying the sky and stars, at times for no other reason than plain curiosity and enjoyment. He never ceased to be amazed at how clear the night sky was in comparison to New Jersey, the area he had come from. There had to be thousands of stars visible from horizon to horizon. On this particular night, they stood out crisply, as though accentuated by a bluish tint.

Lou had retired two years ago at the age of 62 after a long career in industry as a research scientist, specializing in the field of automation. During his 38-year career in the aircraft industry, Lou had witnessed a revolution in science which was truly mind boggling. The advances in technology he had witnessed, and often participated in during his lifetime, were hard to believe. They'd resulted in countless inventions and innovations which contributed to improvements in the quality of life on Earth.

His first exposure to automation was during World War II while he served with the Air Force as an aerial navigator in heavy bombardment. He had been commissioned a 2nd Lieutenant here in Texas at a small air base in Hondo outside of San Antonio. Maybe that first experience at the ripe old age of nineteen had made such an impression that he was bound to return after all these years.

When the end of the war against Japan finally came and he received his honorable discharge after serving with the 20th Air Force, Louis Keck had already made up his mind to pursue a career in automation. He majored in physics and electrical engineering MIT, and after five years, emerged with a master's degree. One month after graduation, he married his high school sweetheart, Katy Robinson, who had been employed as a stenographer by a Boston brokerage firm since her graduation.

Lou's first job as an engineer was in New Mexico at a nuclear weapons development laboratory. The challenge of working in this brand new field of engineering was interesting enough, but he found that the area of specialization was too narrow. Three years later, he accepted a position with an aircraft company as research engineer. Many stimulating and rewarding years would be spent engaged in applied research and development of industrial automation.

As Louis Keck reflected on his past experiences, he felt a sense of relief for having left industry for the position he held where research was once again an enjoyable pursuit with no political strings attached.

Now that raising his children had been successfully completed, the time had come to embark on a new venture. So what if he was more advanced in years than most of his associates? Coming out of retirement to accept a position as a member of the senior staff working on a project as important as controlled fusion, was promising to be one of the most important decisions of his life. Lou had agreed to work on this project with one stipulation: that he be free to pursue any research activity of his choice as long as it was related to the laboratory's goals. Actually, the taming of the fusion process was nowhere in sight, and whether or not it would ever become a reality was anybody's guess. The entire world was in a state of desperation for energy and every possible solution needed to be considered.

As he pondered the Big Bang theory, Lou could not help but wonder how it was possible, without some super intelligent being masterminding the entire process. From his vantage point, man was somewhere within the greatest explosion imaginable and yet able to watch it happen. To explain it in sensible scientific terms was quite something else. During his tenure on Mother Earth, man had discovered laws of physics which governed his existence. Hopefully, many of these (assumed universal) laws should apply when attempting to explain the universe on a mathematical basis. Only the scale of fundamental parameters related to matter, mass, or time, would be different. The possibilities were staggering.

If only someone could develop a usable model of our one and only universe. The database from astronomical observations through the ages is probably greater than for any other branch of science. It stands ready to support or disprove any theories to come along.

All of a sudden the patio door slid open, and Katy poked her head outside.

"Are we going to stay up all night, Dear? Don't you realize what time it is?"

"Sorry about that, Dear," Lou replied. "You know how I get carried away at certain times. This just happens to be one of those nights where the sky could not be ignored. Somehow the key to our very existence has got to be out there."

To this, Katy had a ready made answer which she had used on many previous occasions. "Now you know there's no way you can solve these big problems in one night. Besides, do it on company time and get paid for it. That 8:30 meeting at the lab will be here mighty fast, and you know how hard it is to get you out of bed. Come now, Honey, it's 1:30 in the morning."

"You're right, Dear, no way I can solve this problem tonight. Let's you and I go hit the sack."

3

The trip to Boston for Tom and Molly Curtis had become routine during the past two years. This particular one was no different, though January was not usually a good month for traveling in the state of Maine. And at this point, the excursions held no promise, and Molly felt depressed; her cancer would not go away. She and Tom knew that their options for treatment were running out. The spread of the disease from the original tumor in her left breast to her lungs had been a terrible experience. The last two years had been filled with pain and hurt and hope, and continuous disappointment.

"You know something, Tom? This is probably my last ride to the Gerber Clinic. My condition is terminal- the big C has taken over, and it's only a question of time before they bury me. I know it, you know it, they know it; so, what are we doing this for? Why don't they leave me alone so I can die in peace?"

Tom was driving interstate 295 from Brunswick to Portland where he could pick up the Maine Turnpike heading south. He had taken a day's leave from Kennebec College where he was full professor in the microbiology department. Usually one day was ample time for the round trip and consultations from Boston doctors. If complications developed or Molly was too tired, as had happened once or twice before, they could always put up at a motel along the way.

Tom had gotten accustomed to Molly's remorseful state of mind. He felt so sorry for her, and there was not a damn thing he could do to help her except offer words of encouragement, which at this stage of her condition, seemed meaningless.

Molly had always been a bundle of energy. They had met in Biology 1, sophomore year. Although Tom was three years older than her, because of his service in the Marines during World War II, college had been delayed. Her major was nursing, and he was in the pre-med program at the University of Maine.

Their friendship quickly became a serious relationship. After three years of steady dating, it was obvious that Tom and Molly were well-suited. It came as no surprise when they announced their intentions to get married in the summer of 1975, before Tom entered medical school at Tufts.

The next four years were challenging financially while Tom was in school studying to be a doctor. Molly practiced her profession as a fulltime nurse at Mass General. By carefully budgeting, she was able to support her husband through very tough times. She progressed from a floor nurse to a nursing supervisor in the cardiac section of the big city hospital.

Meanwhile, Tom developed a keen interest in pathology. Course work in microbiology and genetics were especially interesting. Molly and he agreed he should pursue the branch of medicine that would be the most personally satisfying.

By the time he entered his last year of medicine, Tom had made up his mind to be a pathologist. Furthermore, he was determined to be a researcher.

Once he became a full-fledged pathologist, Tom and Molly settled in the Boston area and planned their family. He accepted a staff position at Mass General. They purchased a two-year-old Dutch colonial overlooking the water in Revere Beach, within easy commuting distance from their new home, yet away from the congested city. Years that followed were happy, busy ones for the Curtis family, which grew to include their son, Tom Jr., and daughter Pam.

Proud fathering aside, Tom established quite a reputation in the field of pathology. He frequently presented papers at medical conferences on the latest advances in microbiology and diagnostic methods. During a period of guest lecturing at Tufts, and later as visiting professor of microbiology, Tom came around to the idea of teaching and doing genetic research on a full-time basis in an academic setting. After ten years of experience in a large city hospital, he and Molly decided that the kids were young enough to adapt to a new school and friends. Being from the Portland area, Tom liked the idea of moving back to the state of Maine. Fortunately, he got a position at Kennebec College in Brunswick heading up the biology department and directing their new genetics laboratory.

Acclimation to life as a college professor was enjoyable and came naturally. Tom was totally engrossed in his academic affairs while Molly returned to nursing at Central Maine General in Lewiston.

One morning when Molly was toweling herself off after a shower, she felt an unusual stiffness in her left breast. After probing the area, she felt a small lump. There was no pain, but a definite hardness to it. As an experienced nurse, Molly was not one to panic under such circumstances. She waited for Tom to finish his shower.

"Feel this." She guided his hand to her breast. "This doesn't feel normal to me, what do you think?"

Tom realized Molly was serious, and quickly set aside any notion that she was making advances. "I don't think this is too much to be concerned about, but we should play it safe and schedule a mammogram at the hospital."

"I'll have it done at CMG today while I'm at work," Molly said. And they continued their daily routine to face the new day.

The mammogram was done at CMG shortly after Molly arrived for work. About an hour later, the results were ready, and Molly was called in to Dr. Neff's office for a consultation. He was an expert cancer specialist and believed in being candid with patients.

"Molly, you have a very tiny tumor, about the size of a pea, located in the fatty region of your left breast."

Thus began a new phase in Molly's life that would prove devastating. She had always been an optimist and initially took it in stride.

When it was discovered that the cancer had spread, Molly underwent a radical mastectomy, total removal of her left breast. This was followed by cobalt radiation therapy to burn out the residual infected tissue. A series of chemotherapy treatments administered intravenously was next on the schedule. Molly's stamina and strength gradually ebbed away. Her mental attitude became one of total discouragement, and as progress was not forthcoming, she accepted death as the final outcome.

She had been referred to the Gerber Clinic some time ago and had visited them on numerous occasions. The clinic dealt primarily with residual cancers and cases where conventional treatment methods had been exhausted. "Terminal" patients was a fitting description of the Gerber clientele. The clinic was experimental and its entire effort was devoted to the treatment of cancer using new drugs.

Unfortunately, the cancer had penetrated into Molly's chest cavity and was attaching itself to her left lung. In her own mind, the end was in sight. Molly agreed to participate in one last experiment at the Gerber Clinic, in spite of not having any hope for her own recovery. If any good came of it, it would benefit future cancer patients.

And so, here they were on yet another mission to the cancer clinic as Tom took the entrance ramp to the Maine Turnpike.

Molly managed to doze off for short naps brought on by the heavy sedation she was under. During the past few weeks, part of her medication consisted of morphine shots, administered as needed to relieve pain and discomfort. Tom had given Molly a shot before they left their house, and he expected the effects to last until they arrived at Gerber. He watched her sleep.

We've been through so much together. I love you, Mary. So much. Why is there is nothing I can do for you besides give you your shots? With all the science in the world, how can there be absolutely nothing that will keep you from leaving me? Impossible. That's how it will be to live without you. Unthinkable and impossible.

"Are we almost there, Hon?" Molly woke up as they passed the Revere Beach exit off Interstate 95.

"We'll be at Gerber in another twenty minutes, Moll. Does this look familiar? We had some good years back then, even if we *were* struggling to pay off my college debts," Tom reminisced.

"Ah, yes, we've had so many good years, and we raised two wonderful kids, Tom. We should be grateful for that. What I hate so much about this illness is that I am so helpless and such a burden on you."

"Don't you worry about me, Moll. You've taken care of all of us for so many good years; it's your turn to sit back and be waited on. And we can't give up the hope of something good happening from this experiment." Tom was playing the optimist, but he knew too well that Molly's chances were slim.

Ten minutes later, they pulled into the Gerber parking lot. They were greeted in the lobby by the receptionist and instructed to meet with the others in the auditorium for the 9:00 address by Dr. Stevens, the director of the clinic. When they entered the room, there were several faces they recognized from previous visits.

"Good morning to you all," Dr. Stevens said, opening his talk. "This is beginning to look like an old-home week. I see many of you are no strangers to the Gerber Clinic. Now, let's get to the business at hand, because I'm sure many of you are not feeling comfortable, and there's no reason to make small talk. We, here at Gerber, appreciate your cooperation in helping us set up this experiment. Some of you have come from quite a distance, and I'm sure the trip was no easy matter.

"You've all been briefed, so you have a pretty good idea as to what this new protocol entails. I'm personally grateful that so many of you agreed to participate. I've just been informed that all 226 of the planned test group are present. Thank you. Dr. Goldman will give you a rundown on how we plan to proceed." He motioned Dr. Goldman to take his place at podium.

"Good morning." Dr. Goldman was curt in his manner, but capable and dedicated and did not believe in wasting time. "Everyone here knows about cancer treatment and how in so many cases we seem to be fighting a losing battle. Cancer is unforgiving, and we all know the cure rate is not high, once it has taken a foothold. The key to a cure, and there have been many, has always been early detection. Unfortunately, individuals tolerate pain differently. Consequently, many cases go unnoticed until it is too late. For all of you, I am sure the period of your illness is devastating. Yet, the will to live has kept you hanging by a fine thread- always hoping for that magic cure.

"Our purpose here at Gerber is to try every possible new medicine to see what effect it has on advanced cancers. As you know, our successes have been considerably fewer in number than our failures. However, the fact that we've had some success shows there is hope, and our task will be to continue research to find a protocol that works.

"The margin separating the success and failure of many scientific experiments is sometimes quite narrow, and the interpretation of results can be inconclusive. The treatment of cancer certainly falls in that category. With the help of the statistics department at MIT, we have designed an experiment to help us sort out data and results related to treatment responses in a more meaningful way.

"Before going further, let me tell you that we have obtained a new form of chemo, which is to be administered orally in a pill form. The pharmaceutical house in Holland that developed it has great expectations for effectiveness in treatment. We may be on the verge of discovering a common denominator which will link all cancer therapy to one treatment. The degree of success in treating different types might give us some clue as to how cancer cells develop in the human body. The theory behind the oral intake is to produce a mild ingestion of chemo into the body, thereby creating less of a shock to the patient's metabolism and a greater tolerance for longer term application of the medicine. To make a long story short, we have been selected by the US Food and Drug Administration to evaluate this new form of chemotherapy by group testing, such as you have volunteered for.

"All of you are on file with Gerber in a great amount of detail. We have documented the type of cancer you have, along with the various treatments you have received, your response to each, and finally what the prognosis is. Each of your case histories have been logged into our computer system for identification of similarities and to set up correlations. The final outcome is based on the database and is unbiased.

"Actually, when dealing with a test group as large as this one, we are able to set up almost unlimited numbers of factors that each case can be compared against for fit. The purpose is to pair you with another in the test group whose case history is the most similar to your own. Looking at the audience, I see that you are tired and restless. Let's take a break and plan to reconvene here in a half hour. You will find restrooms off the hallway, and we have coffee and doughnuts in the back of the auditorium."

For a large group of sick people, it was not surprising to see a good number getting pain shots. Among them was Molly; Tom did not waste any time with her shot. When everyone had returned to their seats, Dr. Goldman stood at the podium to resume the talk.

"Now that you seem a bit refreshed, let's pick up where we left off. As I was saying, the object is to pair you up with your twin patient. This has already been done, in order to keep this meeting as short as possible. When you registered this morning, you received a number in range from 1 to 226. Your twin patient has also been assigned a number. For the duration of the test program, you will not know who your twin is. In fact, neither will the Gerber staff. You may think the entire scheme is ridiculous, but there is a method to our madness. Our plan is to carry this out under a cloak of secrecy – a blind experiment. The reason is to avoid misrepresentation of facts as the experiment develops and to eliminate biased judgments pertaining to each case.

"There is one other variable I have not mentioned; however, this one is not a secret to you. I am referring to the use of placebos in our experiment. It would be impossible to detect and then attribute progress to your treatment if we did not have a base of reference for comparison. There lies the reason for setting up pairs among the test group. One of you in each pair will receive the placebo instead of actual medication.

When we first discussed this technique with you, we really did not know what to expect. Sure, many people turned us down, mainly because they did not want to be used as guinea pigs. They certainly cannot be blamed for feeling that way. However, the group gathered here today is remarkable. About all I can say is that you are a gutsy group of people."

At this point, Dr. Goldman paused to look about the auditorium feeling much compassion for these poor, sick people. He thought about how practically everyone here was in a terminal condition, and how at some time prior to this meeting, they'd probably accepted death as the inevitable outcome. Taking part in this experiment was regarded as a final gesture of hope for future victims. He felt that it was better not to dwell on the subject, but to finish describing the upcoming tests.

"We have prepared 226 identical looking packages of the test medication containing a six month supply. The daily dosage in every case will be four tablets with water, one after each meal and one at bedtime. Each package has a unique number stamped on it. As you leave, you will be handed one of these with your assigned number on it. Please start taking this medication today after returning to your homes. Also, whatever medication you have been taking, especially sedatives to relieve pain, you should continue taking as long as your own physician instructs you to do so.

"There is only one person, who happens to be on the MIT teaching staff, who is in possession of the computer file containing all pertinent details. Dr. Stevens will be the only person to override the secrecy rule, if necessary.

"During the next six months, the entire Gerber staff will be anxiously awaiting news of developments so please keep in touch. We told you this would be short, and here it is, 11:10. On behalf of the entire staff, I thank you for your cooperation. Please do not forget to pick up your assigned medical packages on the way out. Goodbye and good luck!"

And so, yet another potential cancer cure was about to be tested, in a unique way. Tom and Molly were not in a conversational mood when they drove back to Brunswick. They had a feeling they had been this route before.

4

It was March, six weeks since Ben Davidson had returned from the hospital after undergoing his heart transplant operation. As he and Mary lay in bed contemplating getting up to face the new day, he said, "Hon, you and I should be thinking about making a baby, now that I am back to normal."

"Wouldn't that be great after all these years; but let's not rush it, Dear. We should find out first what Dr. Armstrong has to say about your condition."

Ben started getting frisky, and Mary sensed that the point of no return was not far off. She laughed as she hopped out of bed and headed for the bathroom before things got out of hand.

"Time to get up," she said. I'll cook us a hearty breakfast, and then we'll head out to the hospital for your ten o'clock appointment."

"I haven't felt this good in years. It's like I'm a new man. I sure am anxious to see what the doc will have in store for me today."

While he showered and shaved, Mary cooked bacon, scrambled eggs, toast, and coffee. She felt so happy that Ben was back to his old self after so many years of sickness during the greater part of their marriage.

Their's had been a strong union in spite of Ben's deteriorating heart condition, discovered ten years ago. The two had met at the NASA Houston Space Center when he started on his first job after graduation from Stanford with a Master's degree in Computer Science. Mary was the group secretary in the Infrared Earth Survey Section where he was assigned. Their relationship blossomed quickly, and within a year they decided to get married. Both wanted children, three to be exact, but settling into his new position would take precedence. In a few short years, he developed a reputation at NASA for being a pretty imaginative scientist. He was instrumental in developing infrared mapping techniques from continuous satellite observations of the Earth's surface. He really enjoyed what he was doing, and there was no question in his mind that he had made the right career choice.

Unfortunately, the onset of Ben's heart problem during his fifth year at NASA put a damper on starting a family. His condition gradually deteriorated, and the decision to take that important step became more remote.

Quite the opposite, his performance on the job got him well-deserved recognition in scientific circles. Infrared monitoring of the Earth's surface was becoming an accepted technique for assessing world food production, identifying sources of atmospheric pollution, and even detecting population trends of many animal life forms. All beings have a unique temperature, and they radiate infrared at a characteristic wavelength. The recently developed high resolution infrared cameras and advanced data processing techniques made it possible to massage this data in many ways. Ben's contributions had been exactly in this area.

"How's our patient been behaving, Mary?" Dr. Armstrong said, greeting them. "Looks to me like he's been in very good hands, judging by his color and general appearance."

"I'd say he is well on the road to recovery, Doctor, and that's no exaggeration," Mary replied with a smile, recalling this morning's episode in bed.

"Let me borrow him for a half hour or so, and we'll find out how good a shape he is really in. Why don't you come with me, Ben, and we'll start with a visit to the lab for a test of your blood count."

Next was a physical exam with particular attention to his heartbeat and breathing sounds. The report from the lab was good. The white corpuscle count was normal, indicating no infection and no sign of impending rejection of his new heart.

The expression on Dr. Armstrong's face was both that of pleasant surprise and yet somewhat questioning. The results were unexpected.

"I am absolutely amazed at your recovery. There is no sign whatsoever to indicate the onset of rejection, which is so common in transplant surgery. Every one of your weekly office visits of the past month has shown nothing out of normal. Frankly, I see no more reason now than a month ago to start anti-rejection procedures. Your case is a medical curiosity in my book, and I recommend close monitoring for a while longer."

"That's great news, Doc, but you still haven't told me if I can return to work at the Space Center." Ben felt full of enthusiasm at the prospect of returning to his old job as head of the demography group.

"In due time, Ben, but first there are clinical tests we'll schedule as a precautionary measure: an ultrasound of the chest, an angiogram, and a fiber optic catheter test which should tell us more about the healing at the interface with your new heart.

"Now, because there is always an outside chance of excessive bleeding at the incision, or even an infection, you should plan for an overnight stay at the hospital.

"Can I answer any questions you may have about these tests? I believe I've explained the procedures to you recently."

"Just one, Doc. Why do we have to be so thorough at this point when my condition is obviously good?"

"I hear what you are saying, but as I said before — you are a medical curiosity. Your progress is phenomenal — and that is out of the ordinary. I'm keeping my fingers crossed that we have not overlooked something. Believe me, Ben, you will probably get written up in the medical journals as one of the few that got himself a perfect match. It's better that we don't take any chances just yet and draw premature conclusions."

"I can buy that; it's just that I'm itching to get back to doing something useful."

"Actually, I'm being extra cautious with you, because from the time your donor heart became available and when it was finally implanted and shocked into operation to become part of your own circulatory system, there was a total elapsed time of close to eight and one half hours. For the heart to be without oxygen for that span of time and then to recover is unheard of. This is what is called ischemic time; past experience has put an upper limit on it of seven hours as the point of no return.

"But the heart appeared viable, and we took a chance in your case because of the difficulty in matching you up with a donor and your rapidly deteriorating condition. It could be that the specified lower storage temperature during transit from Connecticut to Houston allowed the heart organ to survive the extra time."

"From what I hear, Doc, I guess I am a medical marvel."

"Here's another tidbit of information. I was at a medical meeting in London last week to hear the latest in organ transplant technology. You are not the only one making a phenomenal recovery. There have been two cases out of the Stanford Center, one from London, and three cases in Moscow. All reported within the last month and under similar close scrutiny. The one thing you share in common is that all of you received your donor hearts less than two months ago."

"Has there been a medical breakthrough, Doc? Why are we so coincidental?"

"You can never rule out that possibility, but our patient prep and surgical techniques are no different now than they have been, except that we have gotten more practice. Maybe we're getting a little smarter without realizing it.

"Well – enough said for the time being. It's noontime and here we are gabbing away. What do you say we pick up your wife and have lunch in the cafeteria? Then you'll be here in plenty of time for your ultrasound test."

Later that afternoon, good circulation in the heart and lung area was verified. Ben and Mary headed for home, happy with the results thus far.

❧

Two days later, he checked into the hospital for his angiogram and fiber optic probe tests. Here again, the results were excellent – not even a sign of an interface where blood vessels were sutured together.

The next morning, before his discharge, he went to Dr. Armstrong's office for a follow-up appointment. "The radiologist just informed me that you have the circulatory system of a seventeen year old," remarked the doctor, obviously pleased.

"Let's give it one more week before turning you loose. I am plain dumbfounded at your progress — we must have come across a perfect match.

"As far as your sex life is concerned, you can resume normal sexual activity, but avoid overexertion.

"I want to see you again in one month unless you need to see me first. Remember: don't overextend yourself at NASA. Limit your work to half days for the first couple of weeks. Good luck to you."

They shook hands, smiling broadly at their joint accomplishment, and Ben departed.

On the way home with Mary, Ben was deep in thought. *I can't believe it – truly, a new lease on life after such a long ordeal. And it's still not too late to be thinking about raising a family. Mary's biological clock is still running; she's only 34, and her health is excellent. She's wanted to be a mom for so long, and now the obstacle is gone. With good luck, her wish can come true.*

And talk about luck – NASA keeping my job open for four months is pretty lucky. At least I've been able to stay in touch with my bosses and members of my group. I think I'm pretty much up-to-date on current activities. It's going to be exciting and meaningful; the government upheavals in Eastern Europe and the massive changes in Russia are bound to affect world population trends. There is no doubt that demographic studies will move to the forefront in the coming years. Awesome that funding to develop the application of infrared monitoring by a polar orbiting satellite is being given top priority.

I know my group can develop computer software to sort out the massive amount of data, separate infrared components due to human emissions, and produce a global map of human population. And since polar orbits provide world coverage of the Earth's surface, the map will continuously update as the Earth rotates beneath the satellite.

Ben was in a state of anxiety and anticipation; this type of effort was exactly in the realm of his expertise. *I don't know how I'll only do half days – but is that necessary if what I'm doing is more pleasure than work?*

5

Taming of the fusion process had been one of the top priorities on the list of government-funded research programs for the past fifty or so years. In fact, the quest for controlled fusion had been a worldwide goal pursued by most of the technically-advanced countries with a dire need for energy to support their sophisticated lifestyles.

There were two major reasons for the present concern. First, the conventional sources of energy were rapidly becoming depleted. Second, these same natural sources of energy, including nuclear energy, were proving to be polluters of the environment and had reached life-threatening levels.

Therein lay the purpose for the frantic research activity taking place at numerous institutions of higher learning, as well as industry, throughout the country.

The weekly Monday morning meeting of the fusion group had just assembled in their usual conference room with most participants still carrying their Styrofoam cups of coffee. Professor Charlie Stafford was the team leader and very much at home in the informal atmosphere.

"Ladies and gentlemen, let's get the meeting underway because we have several items up for discussion. First of all, let me briefly summarize where the scientific community stands today in fusion research.

"We've learned a hell of a lot about hydrogen fusion during these past few years, but we have yet to figure out a way to harness it for useful power production. What I've just said could be the opening statement at any meeting such as this one- or wherever there is ongoing fusion research. The fact of the matter is that we all know about fusion.

"However, little is known about creating the necessary conditions that would make possible a steady-state release of fusion energy. We are all familiar with the cold fusion in a bottle reported on several years back. That didn't work simply because the process is far more complex than it was purported to be, but we have to admit — it was a novel approach.

"After each failed attempt, we seem to come back to ground zero for a fresh start in a different direction."Does anyone care to comment on what I've just said? What are your thoughts on the subject, Lou? You are new with us, but I imagine you bring much wisdom to the group with your many years of experience."

"You're putting me on the spot, Charlie. But so what, I'm not afraid to put in my two cents," Lou replied. Scientists around the table laughed. "First of all, where I come from and with a background in both science and engineering, I try to see things from a perspective that falls somewhere in the middle. That may put me in no-man's land, but if you are willing to listen, I will give you my point of view.

"Learning how to obtain useful energy from fusion processes is probably the most challenging problem ever tackled by mankind, as we all know. The best minds in the world have been working on this since the end of World War II. On the scientific side, physicists and allied scientists have done a commendable job analyzing and defining the process itself and then proving their theories experimentally in a laboratory.

"Meanwhile, engineers have been devising ways to scale up these experiments to yield practical amounts of power. So far, the power to operate these sophisticated experiments has been far greater than the power produced. The break-even point has yet to be reached. The hardware to support each succeeding phase, as power output escalates, is growing more complex and power consuming. At this point, many of our colleagues wonder if the path being followed is leading anywhere.

"There is no question that much has been learned and progress is being made every day. Knowledge has always been a direct result of research.

"However, maybe we should expend more effort on building computer models that would apply new theories and data coming out of our laboratories. These models could be tests to simulate actual fusion reactions.

"Now, please don't misunderstand me, this type of activity has always been going on. All I'm suggesting is that we make more use of computer test models and we track the simulated reaction as it progresses. I'm sure that this type of effort would be looked at as reinvention of the wheel, and probably rightly so — but there's always a chance that something was missed or incorrectly analyzed previously, and the test model would uncover that fact.

"Those are my thoughts on the subject. Now you can take pot shots and prove me wrong."

"I like the suggestion, but isn't this just a rehash of what's been going on?" came the remark of a team member at the end of the table. "We make use of the computers every step of the way to predict changes in results. Where is your approach any different?"

Charlie Stafford came to Lou's rescue. "If I get the picture right, Lou is proposing a computer modeling of a *full scale reaction* as opposed to day-to-day usage of the computer, as a guide to running the experiment. Isn't this what you had in mind, Lou?"

"That's about right, Charlie. But please keep in mind that I was thinking out loud, and what I said can be interpreted in many ways."

"I think the idea has merit," Charlie said, "and should be considered a new task here at the institute. The immediate problem is that there is no allowance for funding a new effort on our existing contract. We can contact the program monitor at DOE in Washington for a visit as soon as possible to discuss additional funding; and Lou — I'm appointing you project leader as of now."

Charlie Stafford was not one to mince words. He found the direct approach was the most effective way to drive a point home.

"Gee thanks, Charlie. I have a feeling this was a setup, and I walked right into it," Lou replied with a smile.

"

Why do you suppose we pulled you out of retirement, Lou? System modeling and simulation is where your expertise lies; and with your background, you should be able to interface with both sides of the fence.

"We're looking for fresh approaches. For starters, let's take a look at a thermo-nuclear reaction like the H-bomb itself. At least, that's a process we know works, even though it is uncontrolled. Why don't we concentrate on producing a computer model of the reaction distribution within the fusion envelop? We're dealing with an uncontrolled explosion, but we might be able to gain some insight on how it progresses as a function of time.

"Then, let's examine the mechanism that causes the reaction to snuff itself out. That's an area that should prove interesting — looking at the tail-end of the process when our efforts in recent years have been on how to initiate it."

"That's a pretty big order, Charlie, but it sure looks compelling. We'll start with some simple-minded approaches to a reacting vessel. From there, hopefully, we can progress to something more representative of an actual fusion reactor. I just hope we don't end up delving into Pandora's Box and going around in circles."

"Nobody's asking for guarantees, Lou. The whole point to this effort is to develop a new way to look at the problem. Your past experience with system analysis could prove useful in identifying areas where more research is required."

"I'm willing to give it my best shot, but I'll be looking for input from all you experts to avoid going off on a tangent, OK?" The group nodded their assent.

"Good — that's one item settled on the agenda. You have full use of the facilities, Lou. In preparing the estimate for your level of effort and costs, don't forget to factor in the expensive machine time for the Cray super computer, because I'm sure you'll be needing it.

"Now, let's proceed to the next item up for discussion."

The remainder of the meeting went quickly as each team member reported on the previous week's progress or setbacks on tasks of the government contract.

Later in his office, Lou was already deep in thought, laying out his own plan of attack. First, he had to call Katy. "Honey, I took a giant step for mankind today."

"Well, don't keep me in suspense. What happened at the big meeting?"

"I got myself the new position as team leader, can you imagine — at my age? Actually, I'll be doing what I was hired for. It just took some time to materialize."

"Congratulations anyway, Dear. I hope you don't spend all your free time gazing at the stars from now on. What do you say we go out to dinner tonight to celebrate the occasion?"

"Sounds like a good idea. I should be home by 5:30. OK? I have to go because I'm meeting Charlie in a few minutes for lunch. See you later."

During the rest of the day, Lou's mind was engaged in how to proceed with this new venture. *Hmmm, my past experiences modeling systems had nothing to do with mathematically representing a fusion reaction. Although, the rules aren't expected to be much different. The equations of motion of bodies (kinematics), and the fundamental laws of motion are going to apply in any situation. The laws of physics will never be violated, no matter how large or small the parts in question are.*

Like Charlie said at the meeting — why not start with something we know works? It could be thought of as a miniature Big Bang, the predominant theory of how the universe was born.

In any case, the fusion process is made possible by the compression of hydrogen nuclei until these same nuclei are close enough to each other to allow them to fuse together into helium. The release of fusion energy at that instant will stir up other nuclei in the reactor to produce even more fusion energy. The explosive reaction will continue for as long as containment can be maintained. The H-Bomb is a man made gadget where the compressive force to trigger fusion is produced by an imploding fission bomb using either uranium or plutonium. In such a case, the fission bomb totally encloses the hydrogen core, which is subjected to tremendous compression once the onset of fission is triggered. Containment is achieved dynamically for a small instant in time when the forces, due to fission, are directed inwardly to a focal point at the center of the core, as well as outwardly. That briefest amount of time is sufficient to bring about fusion.

The Big Bang, by comparison, was probably a more natural phenomenon and a onetime event that will be forever speculated about. One can imagine the Creator seeding the voids of space with hydrogen and putting into effect the laws of physics to preamble the main event. Maybe then he allowed the process to begin. Gravitational forces took over and the free fall of the hydrogen molecules commenced. Motion towards the center of mass increased almost imperceptibly at first, but with time, a race was on to the center of gravity to create the newborn universe. The resulting increase in density of hydrogen nuclei at the center ignited the Big Bang. The entire process was over in a small fraction of a second, but all the elements were created during that minute instant in time when the expanding universe was created.

Lou made up his mind to make the Big Bang his first model.

6

Molly had mixed emotions about participating in the cancer therapy test program ever since she and Tom had returned home from their last visit to the Gerber Clinic in early January. *I'll be a guinea pig in an experiment; I'm deteriorating and might not even be receiving treatment for my illness. What if I'm on — placebos? What a way to spend my remaining days on Earth. Tom must be so tired of putting up with me, and he's got to know my condition is hopeless.* More than once in the past few weeks, she had thought about taking her own life. It would be such a relief for her family to know she was out of her misery. In her mind, it was not fair to be such a burden on her loved ones.

The truth was quite the opposite. Tom was a dedicated husband and he adored his wife. The experience of seeing her gradually waste away was killing him. It took all the courage he could muster to act optimistic when in her presence. Pam and Tom, Jr. were the same way when they came home to visit. Pam was living in Boston with her husband, George, who was finishing his senior year in pre-law. She visited her mother every two weeks or so. Tom, Jr. was in his first year of medicine at John Hopkins, and his visits were not as frequent due to his greater distance from home. He made time to get home for short weekends, as often as possible.

Knowing she had a loving family was what kept Molly going. Each was devoted to her and did their best to cheer her up. She couldn't convince herself to take the road of cowardice and leave them with such a legacy.

For the past two months, Tom had taken Molly to the local hospital for a chest tap to remove fluid buildup between the lungs and rib cage.

This was a necessary procedure or else she'd die of suffocation. The frequency of visits was about once every two weeks and required an overnight stay each time.

On her last visit two weeks ago, the quantity of fluid extracted was considerably less than usual. The hospital resident had been somewhat perplexed: a lung cancer patient's condition worsened with time, the opposite should happen.

Today, Tom got home from the college at the usual time for lunch and then going to the hospital for the chest tap at two thirty. As he opened the front door, he heard coughing coming from the downstairs bathroom.

"This is strange," he muttered to himself. Of late, Molly had become a recluse in her bedroom on the second floor. "What's the matter, Moll, aren't you more comfortable staying in bed? Are you alright? Can I do something to help you?"

"I thought I'd prepare your lunch today as a surprise, Hon," she replied, coming out of the bathroom and hugging him. "It's all set up in the kitchen."

Tom was floored. *Could her condition be improving? No — it couldn't be — she's much too far along to even consider that possibility.*

"I was just getting over a coughing spell as you came in, but I'm okay now. Seems like I'm able to breathe better lately."

"I understand, Sweetie, but you shouldn't be out of bed unless someone is here to help you. Don't worry about me getting my own lunch — I'm an old hand at it by now."

Tom had his regular cup of soup and a sandwich, only this time it had already been prepared for him. Molly sipped on a glass of fruit juice while he ate.

"You haven't lost your touch, Moll. That was better than what I've been eating lately. I'll put away these dishes and then help you get dressed for the ride to the hospital."

"What would you say if we canceled my appointment, Tom? I really don't think I need a tap today, and besides, it's so darn uncomfortable."

Tom had always known Molly to have a good head on her shoulders as a nurse, and her request was not farfetched. On the other hand, if she thought there was the least little sign of improvement in her condition after such a devastating illness, she would likely overestimate its significance and could set herself up for a letdown later on. He would have to be on his guard not to allow such a development; yet he didn't want to discourage her.

"I'll tell you what, Sweetheart, we can cancel your appointment if you promise me you will stay in bed for the rest of the day. You know this is serious business. Let's tuck you in, and I'll give you your morphine shot before heading back to the college."

"I have a second request, Hon. Let's skip the morphine shot — I want to see if I can get along without it. Besides, I'm not in pain right now, and why take a chance on becoming a dope fiend."

Now Tom really felt backed into a corner. Something was not right. Molly had been in such discomfort during the past several months; she never refused relief.

After helping Molly to bed, he kissed her goodbye. *What is going on?*

"Call me if you change your mind. I can be here in fifteen minutes."

On the ride back to campus, Tom was deep in thought considering the significance of this latest development. *Could I be overreacting? Could Molly be getting a new chemo and it's doing its job? What a breakthrough this could be for cancer treatment.*

The thought of getting a chemical analysis of one of her pills had gone through his mind more than once since their last visit to the Gerber Clinic. From a professional point of view, it was not the ethical thing to do, however, since he was so close to the patient — his own wife — he could easily justify finding out on his own if Molly was getting the real thing — or placebos. Then again, chemical analysis would not necessarily provide a sure shot answer either. Sometimes placebos were chemically camouflaged with trace amounts of a wide variety of elements so as to make any tampering with analysis inconclusive.

After today's development, Tom convinced himself that Molly really was undergoing chemotherapy, and her first reaction was favorable.

Back home, Molly had thoughts of her own. *Am I taking the real pills — or might they be placebos? Fifty percent of the test group is getting the true medicine. And how is my twin patient doing? It doesn't matter; I'll most likely never find out the results of how many, if any, of the 225 other patients in the test group survive the experiment.*

What a modus operandi — all for the purpose of ensuring unbiased judgments and conclusions at the end of the six-month test period. Medical science can be so devious and cruel at times when executing its method of operation. We are nothing more than data stats, and most of us will end up dying anyway. She felt bitterness when she reminded herself that half of the test group had already been handed death sentences; and out of the remainder, some might live in their misery for a few months or possibly a year longer. *Is it at all worth the effort?*

So far, the change in Molly had been gradual; she didn't suspect what was happening. After being ill for so long, first with breast cancer and then when it spread to her left lung, she had accepted death as the ultimate answer to her problems.

She was a strong-willed person, outright stubborn at times, and came to a decision. *I'm going to stop using morphine.* Like an alcoholic who wants to break the habit by first getting rid of all liquor or beer in their surroundings, Molly poured every bottle of narcotic down the sink and destroyed all hypodermic needles in the house.

Tom called home a couple of times during that afternoon to check on Molly.

"Hey, Sweetheart, do you feel like you need some relief yet?" he asked.

"No thanks, Hon. I'm okay. I'll see you later," Molly replied, keeping her plan to herself.

When he arrived home for dinner, Molly was already craving her next shot. It was pretty obvious, seeing how restless she had become in just a few hours.

"Tom, you've got to help. I don't want any more morphine." This is how she greeted him when he came in the front door. No question about it, she was frantic.

"Yes, but you don't need to endure all that pain, Moll. Listen to me. We all love you and can't bear to see you suffer so much." Tom hugged her and did his best to comfort her.

Escalating into nearly a state of hysteria, Molly shrieked, "I don't care what you say. I'm not in pain right now, and I don't want any more of that god-damned stuff. It's poisoning me, and I'm scared of it."

Tom had visions of his wife turning into a raving maniac. This episode was just the beginning, but for now, he'd have to go along with her wishes.

"You realize that you'll need 24 hour care. It'll get pretty nasty, and you'll be in a straitjacket to ensure you don't hurt yourself. Are you prepared to do that?"

"Yes, Hon; let's get a nurse here tonight. And promise me – no more morphine, no matter what I say!"

The next two weeks were a nightmare. Molly had a specially trained nurse to help her go through the drug withdrawal. Most of the time, she was strapped in bed, experiencing fits of anger, crying spells, and swearing sessions where she yelled out every cuss word known.

"Please, I'm begging you, put me out of my misery. I was wrong, I need it," she'd plead to the nurse or Tom. It was horrific, but even at her worst times, they made sure she was on her chemotherapy regime of four pills per day.

Molly's condition stabilized near the end of the second week of withdrawal. She gradually became herself and the worst of the battle had been fought.

Tom had worried about his wife falling into a depression once she was totally free of her meds. But a miraculous occurrence totally vaporized that fear. Her condition – both mental and physical – improved. Gone were the coughing spells that seemed to last forever. She no longer had shortness of breath and was able to breathe deeply.

"Oh my God, Tom! I think I may finally beat the cancer!" Molly gushed to her husband. Her happiness was palpable.

"Molly, you might – it's been two months since we were at Gerber, and it seems like you're making progress." Tom was cautious in his own elation. False hopes that had ended in utter disappointment were too recent. But he was careful to hide his doubts from Molly, whose entire outlook on life returned to optimism.

On the weekend of March 7, Molly's birthday, their kids visited. Radiant, she smiled like the mother they'd known, while she opened her gifts, each celebrating her improved health and the Curtis family's love of the outdoors.

"Pam — what a lovely warm up suit — and my favorite pink color too. Thank you so much, Dear." The two of them hugged as tears of gratitude appeared in each one's eyes.

"You really expect me to do a lot of hiking now, don't you, Tommy? These Reebok sneakers couldn't be more appropriate, because I plan to start walking as soon as your dad turns me loose. Thanks so much, son — come and kiss your proud mother."

Last but not least were a pair of airline tickets from Tom for a getaway week to Cancun, Mexico, dated May 19, after the end of the spring term at Kennebec College. Molly broke down in tears of happiness as Tom held her in his arms. Each one of her presents was like a vote of confidence from her family to hurry up and get better. She knew she'd treasure that day, no matter what ultimately occurred.

During the following weeks, Molly regained much of her strength and started a mild exercise program to tone up her muscles. Her appetite returned, and she gained a few pounds which headed her towards her original weight.

"Tom," she said one night, "I'm convinced that the medicine I'm taking is for real. I haven't felt this good in such a long time. It's a miracle, like the cancer never happened. Here it is just three and a half months into chemotherapy and I feel cured."

Tom just looked at her with eyes glistening. He couldn't argue. What she was saying seemed to be true.

"I'm going to get back in good physical condition for our trip to Cancun. Remember how much we enjoyed visiting there three years ago? I'll be able to do everything this time around: tennis, swimming in the warm Gulf waters, lounging on the pure white beaches, visiting the Mayan ruins, going to the bull fights — well, maybe not that, once was enough — but we can go out on the town for dinner and dancing. Tequila slammers! Remember! Those were so fun to drink."

"How could I forget?" Tom said.

"How can I thank you for such a wonderful birthday present?"

"It's a gift for me too," he said. "That we get to go on vacation again…" his voice broke.

In all his years studying pathology and medicine, Tom had never experienced a phenomenon so extremely rare. Never had he witnessed such a remarkable recovery. It had to be a major breakthrough for cancer research. He felt so thankful that his dear wife was undergoing what appeared to be a complete cure.

His curiosity got the best of him, and he scheduled Molly for a biopsy at the hospital.

When the results came back negative, Tom did a recheck on the test at the school's pathology lab. The results were again — negative.

He and Molly were so excited, they had to break the good news to somebody. Why not call the Gerber Clinic? The next morning Tom called Dr. Stevens at the clinic to tell him about the results.

"This is very good news, Dr. Curtis. You and Molly must be overjoyed at such a turnabout. Actually, we have received similar news from some of the other members of the test group which is very encouraging."

"Should we continue Molly's chemo regimen for the remainder of the test period, Doctor Stevens?"

"Definitely, please continue the same dosage until her supply is used up. We were instructed to set the treatment period at no less than six months, both by the supplier and the USDA."

"Incidentally, my wife and I are so encouraged over her recovery that I went ahead and scheduled a week's trip to Cancun in late May. The expectation of that trip is proving to be an excellent morale builder for her after what she's been through. That's not a problem, is it?"

"No, No. If she is looking forward to it and feels good, I'll leave that decision up to you, Dr. Curtis. It's a great idea. Make sure that she doesn't get too much exposure to the sun because it could have an adverse effect on her recovery. I'm glad you called with the good news, Doctor. Hopefully, I'll be talking with you at our July meeting. Goodbye now."

Molly continued to get stronger. She was able to venture out of doors for long walks — unattended. Actually, she was getting a bit fidgety for lack of things to do — a sure sign that she was well on the road to a full recovery.

7

The decade came to be known as the period of great advance in medicine. Hardly a day went by without the news media reporting on a spectacular recovery from an incurable disease. Molly Curtis and Ben Davidson were not isolated cases of total healing from serious maladies. Stories of miraculous recoveries of terminally ill people were prime topics for discussion. Case histories of cured patients were front page news and swept through social media. The entertainment industry took advantage of these stories by producing documentaries for TV broadcasting.

An air of euphoria took hold; most people felt satisfied with the quality of life available to everyone. Even the incidence of new cancers seemed to be decreasing. Perhaps typical, people became complacent about taking care of their health. An attitude emerged that no matter what happened — medical science would take care of it; genetics of the human species appeared better understood. The long sought goal of total elimination of deadly diseases and the development of body maintenance technology, allowing worn out parts to be replaced, seemed to have been reached. Advances in organ transplant medicine were significant too, with success rates higher than ever. The selection criteria for matching recipients to donors of most body organs was so fine-tuned, perfect matches were practically guaranteed.

On the other hand, the medical community observed these new developments with skepticism. Why all of a sudden so much success in curing these dreaded diseases? Past advancements in medicine had been painstakingly slow due to the extremely complex workings of the human body. Healing patients had required the joint efforts of numerous specialized branches of medicine supported by each of the allied sciences. Could it be there was finally a payoff for all the research, time, and money that had gone into the treatment of cancer, the most feared of all diseases? The same could be said about organ transplant surgery. Had they reached the point where worn out or sick body organs could be replaced by healthy ones without having to worry about organ rejection?

Something was happening in the world of which man was unaware. The realization that a strange phenomenon was indeed taking place had not taken hold yet. Understanding it would prove to be something else.

8

Jim Coleman had been vice president at Consolidated Industries Corporation for three years, when he was suddenly terminated during a reduction of unproductive staff at senior levels. Jim's mentor, Ed, a longtime friend from his early days at CIC, had advanced through the corporate hierarchy and brought Jim along as he advanced through the company ranks.

Since graduating with an engineering degree, the doughy-bodied, redhead had worked his entire career for CIC at the company's research center. He acquired formidable credentials during his tenure of twenty years, groomed for ever more responsible positions until he reached his peak level. As fate would have it, Jim's mentor was advised to take early retirement, and Jim had to fare on his own.

Unfortunately, he had risen in the company ranks — on false pretenses. His technical and management skills were actually quite limited. With his forte in writing, he had become a skilled report writer, which had made him appear proficient to his superiors. His other strength was identifying program failures – albeit too late: well along in the process and right before they occurred. But he always had a fall guy among his subordinates – and that person would get laid off. This pattern of performance did not go totally unnoticed at the corporate office. Jim was a classic example of the popular cliché called "The Peter Principle": A person will rise in the ranks of an organization to his level of incompetence; and either he will stay at that level – or eventually get fired.

During the cutbacks at CIC, Jim's 'trusted other,' Alec Steiner, had also been fired. The two, fast friends since meeting at a management seminar years earlier, set up appointments for interviews at a number of large firms for positions as efficiency experts, but their notoriety from CIC followed them. Politely, they were informed in every case that they were overqualified for the positions.

The possibility of a study contract with Uncle Sam looked like a last recourse, but— how to achieve this?

While surfing trade journals for ideas, Jim spotted an article in the *Commerce Daily* on Global Science Trends by none other than Dr. Lucas Fieldstone. Could this be the same Lucas Fieldstone employed at CIC years ago? He'd left on a sort of unpleasant note— ego problems.

"Let's pay our friend a visit. He can probably give us some insight on how to get a government study contract," Jim proposed.

The very next day Jim and Al hopped a plane to Washington.

"Well, well, what do you know? Seems like fate has drawn us together again. What are we up to this time? It can't be a reconnection with CIC? What are you looking for?" Luke asked, arrogance intact.

"We don't work for CIC as I'm sure you've heard through the grapevine, Luke. We're here on a friendly visit to see how it is working for Uncle Sam. You seem to be quite successful in your current position. Maybe you can tell us how difficult it is to get a study contract," Jim said.

"If you are looking for a shortcut to a contract, that is not legal, and you could be arrested for using insider information." Luke enjoyed himself, watching the two squirm in their seats.

Alex looked embarrassed, absently rubbing his prematurely balding head, and Jim tried hard to hide his irritation.

After a short pause, Luke continued, "If you guys are looking for work, I know of a sure-fire agency that's in need. With you popping in unannounced today, luck may have dealt us three a golden opportunity. How about it?"

Jim and Alex were stunned.

"What the hell are you talking about?" said Jim, suspicious from the get-go.

"Now, calm down, I'm telling you about an opportunity that could be a moneymaker for the three of us." He actually looked on the level.

42

"I've been thinking of starting my own research and consulting firm, and this might be the perfect time to do it."

Luke had a hunch the two were desperate for work, and that he could use them as underlings. Jim's talent for generating reports could be a beneficial addition to his bag of tricks, and Al could be the group gofer.

"My terms are as follows: my take — 51% control, and I am the boss. The remaining 49% is yours to divvy up as you wish. And if you agree, we can sign papers ASAP.

"Have you been reading the papers? Miracle cures of deadly diseases and successful organ transplants are reported daily. The Office of the Surgeon General must be in a quandary whether or not this is a hoax. I'm considering an unsolicited proposal to the office to make a study of the subject; I have a reliable contact there who could expedite such a deal."

"We need a moment to confer," Jim said.

"Sure," Luke said. "I'll get a cup of coffee and be right back."

"Can you believe this?" Al said, once Luke had left the room.

"I know," Jim said. "Even if I don't trust the guy, it's a pretty fantastic offer."

"I'm tempted, but what about his rep?" Al said.

"Pompous ass," said Jim. "But we have nothing else brewing…could be a way to drum up opportunities for ourselves in the future."

Al waited, knowing that it was up to Jim to decide.

"Let's go for it," Jim said.

Luke strode back into the office.

"Well, we had a couple other prospects, but this is intriguing…so we'll sign the papers," Jim said.

"Good," Luke said. "First off, I'll need a proposal in hand no later than a week from today. Then I'll handle it from there. In the meantime, I'll close my current activity with Uncle Sam and get my lawyer to set up a contract ready for our signatures. I'm depending on you, Jim, to do a first class job here." Luke was thrilled to have a couple of gophers to do his work.

One week later, Luke checked the draft proposal, making sure he was listed as the principal investigator with Jim and Al as his assistants. He then hand-delivered the completed document to his contact at the Office of the Surgeon General.

Two weeks after that, Luke was summoned back to the Office of the Surgeon General, and walked out with a contract worth $600K.

Could this be real? In spite of themselves, Jim and Al were impressed with their new boss. Maybe he *was* a shrewd salesman. The contract stipulated a duration of six months starting immediately; the urgency to find answers was there in black and white.

9

The next four months were a hectic period of travel, setting up appointments, interviewing medical personnel and patients, and compiling enormous amounts of data to be sorted out for computer entry.

Luke, Jim, and Al each had their own travel itineraries in a three-pronged effort to accumulate as much information, as quickly as possible. The major medical centers in the continental United States were covered by Jim; Luke visited institutions in Europe, and Al flew off to the Far East.

Included on Jim's agenda were the Gerber Cancer Clinic in Boston and the Houston Medical Center in Texas. His data-gathering mission was well received at Gerber after he briefed the staff on the purpose of the study. He was given access to all files containing case histories of cancer patients.

Dr. Stevens, head of the clinic, met with Jim to caution him about disclosing information considered proprietary within Gerber.

"You must realize, Mr. Coleman, that we have ongoing projects that we prefer to keep confidential because of the uncertainty of final results. Being a test clinic, we have been chartered on many occasions by the US government and pharmaceutical houses to evaluate certain drugs for the treatment of cancer. As you know, we perform these evaluations by group testing actual cancer patients."

"I understand what you're getting at, Dr. Stevens," Jim said. "My purpose in visiting Gerber is to acquire patient profile data and nothing else. Please feel confident that we will not make public any work that you prefer to keep under wraps. By the same token, we are also doing an office study and would appreciate confidentiality for the duration of our program as well."

"I'm glad we share an attitude of respect for the purpose of each other's work. Now, I'd like to tell you about one of our present experiments at Gerber. We are evaluating the latest chemotherapy on a test group of terminally ill cancer patients. Only this time, we are also using placebos. We have enlisted 226 participants who range in age, gender, and ethnicity. Cancer is the unfortunate equalizer." He went on to give a few details of the remarkable study in progress.

"The experiment is being done blind. Medical staff, as well as patients, are unaware of who is receiving the real medication. If you are wondering how this is possible, we had considerable help from the MIT department of statistics in designing the experiment.

"As I'm sure you can appreciate, Jim, cancer is such an evasive disease; its own progression in a victim is extremely difficult to quantify. Somehow, a benchmark has to be set up from which we can make comparisons and draw meaningful conclusions.

"After a six-month testing period, our medical staff will reexamine these patients and hopefully learn more about the treatment's effectiveness.

"Progress in the medical field is probably just as hard to come by, if not more so, than in the physical sciences, which has been my area of expertise. Quite often, truth is buried in unrelated and insignificant data. Lab experiments need to be designed in such a way that facts can be extracted from a mix of information and plain old noise. Identification of definitive causality and relationships is our greatest challenge."

"I am very interested in the final outcome of your experiment, Dr. Stevens, and I wish you the best of luck."

"Thank you, Jim, and please feel free to use salient information from our files."

The data gathering process was simplified and expedited by the use of an in-house computer which generated printouts of patient data and compiled cumulative patient profiles on a zip drive for Jim.

After being granted permission from the clinic to interview some of the patients participating in the test program, Jim traveled through

New England, visiting with sick people from all walks of life. Some of the meetings were depressing – seeing deteriorating conditions and imminent deaths of individual patients. Others were not available, as they had passed on. A sizable number of the test group appeared well on their way to recovery.

The last of Jim's visits was with Molly Curtis in Brunswick, Maine. She was the 21st Gerber patient interviewed. It was April 4th, two weeks into phase one of the contract.

Damn, thought Jim. *I only have four months to gather data. At this rate, I'm going to fall considerably short of my goal of twenty-five thousand cases.*

As he pulled into the Curtis's driveway, he was greeted by Molly, just returning from her daily walk downtown. She looked athletic in a pink warm-up suit and matching sneakers. He rolled down the window.

"Are you the gentleman from the government survey team?"

"Why, yes; I'm looking for a Molly Curtis, does she live here?"

"I'm the one you're looking for. Dr. Stevens told my husband and me that you would be coming by. Why don't you come in? It's still a bit chilly outside. My husband should be home from the college any minute."

"I'm Jim Coleman, by the way, and my survey team represents the Surgeon General's Office," Jim said, getting out of the car. "You don't look like someone with a terminal illness."

Hmm, Molly thought, *one of those people who has no filter on what comes out of his mouth.* She smiled as they shook hands. Hers was a firm grip, which surprised Jim, because of her illness. Quite the opposite, Molly was taken aback by the limp, clammy hand of Jim.

Once in the house, Jim was told to make himself comfortable in the living room while Molly got a pot of coffee going in the kitchen.

"So," Jim began, "are you trying any kind of healing techniques that fall outside of the medication protocol at the Clinic? Chinese herbs? Homeopathic remedies?"

"Oh, no," Molly said. "When I agreed to be part of the study, I committed wholeheartedly to comply with their strict requirements and rules.

I'm just beyond grateful that since becoming a participant, my health has done a turn around."

Tom pulled into the driveway. "Oh, here's Tom."

Molly greeted her husband at the door with a hug and kiss and introduced him to Jim.

"So, you're the man from Washington we've been expecting?" Jim said, shaking hands.

"To start with, Dr. Curtis, Mrs. Curtis, I am not a government employee. My firm is under contract with the Surgeon General's Office to perform a worldwide survey of medical patients, ill with disease, usually considered hopeless. Please accept my sincere apology for being so blunt, but I know of no other way to state my purpose."

Sensitivity obviously not his forte, Molly spoke quickly. "Don't feel embarrassed, Mr. Coleman. It's a fact that I was gravely ill with lung cancer, but I am in a state of remission, as Tom will confirm. Please, call me Molly. We are very informal in this house."

"Well, you certainly must be reacting positively," Jim said, writing some notes down on a clipboard.

"Molly is undergoing rapid improvement, which we are thrilled about. Her recovery is miraculous."

"That is exactly the purpose of this survey, Dr. Curtis. There have been many reports of recoveries similar to Molly's that were unheard of until recently. My colleagues and I are working to accumulate enough case histories to identify a common denominator."

"I presume you'll be performing correlation tests against many parameters in the patient's personal profile. Those analyses can be misleading unless you acquire a pretty large database. What numbers are you aiming for, Jim?"

"Our goal is in the neighborhood of a hundred thousand case histories. That may seem overly ambitious, but we feel it is entirely feasible given the number of large medical institutions in the world. Most data is already computerized and ready to be queried. A marvelous development in technology, isn't it, Dr. Curtis? I was able to get 783 case histories through Gerber alone. We are confident that the larger our database, the greater our chances of success. Our survey team has many years of industry experience working with information theory." Jim didn't even try to control the tone of pomposity in his response. He wasn't about to let some country bumpkin teaching at a hick school tell him how to run his business.

"Don't base all your conclusions on statistical analyses, Jim, even though you may be working with a large database. Computers aren't going to do it all for you as I'm sure you must realize. Let me give you a word of caution about statistical techniques. They can be very misleading if results are not interpreted correctly and you happen to stress parameters that are actually insignificant."

"Where are you headed next, Jim?" Molly interjected. She sensed a confrontation brewing between Jim and her husband.

"Mass General Hospital. Then I'll be traveling across the country, stopping at major medical centers all the way to the West Coast. I'll make a return pass by a different route with a stop at the Houston Medical Center and then back to New York, John Hopkins, and finally, home-base in Washington with a last stop at Georgetown."

"That's a pretty ambitious itinerary, Jim," Dr. Curtis said. "Do you plan to visit with other individual cases like you are today?"

"Only a few. We are under strict time constraints, and that would be too time consuming. Personal visits are small in number – to satisfy a different requirement on our contract.

"Speaking time constraints, it's important that I maintain my schedule, and besides, I've already taken up enough of your time. I have to make it to Boston tonight if I'm to keep my appointment with Mass

General in the morning. I want to thank you both for spending this time with me."

"Can we interest you in staying over for dinner, Jim?" Molly asked.

"No, thank you for your hospitality, but I really must be on my way."

After Jim had left, Molly breathed a sigh of relief that this man who presented himself as an infallible expert turned down her invitation – any further discussion of the survey program would surely have escalated into a heated argument. As it turned out, both she and Tom shared the same eerie feelings about their visitor. It was like talking to a machine whose sole purpose was to accumulate data, regardless of the quality. He seemed so intent on obtaining the largest number of names possible, as if that was the single most important goal of the study.

The completion of Jim's survey of the Gerber cancer research program was one milestone reached out of a long list of places yet to be visited. During the next two months, he criss-crossed the country visiting major medical institutions. In many places, though extended ample courtesy and cooperation by his hosts, Jim did not impress the professionals he was dealing with. They were civil towards him, but mainly because he represented a branch of the US government, and that's why data files of case histories were made available.

One of the last ports of call on Jim's itinerary was Houston, Texas, where he met with staff members at the Medical Center.

In Dr. Robert Armstrong's office, he described the purpose of his mission, and in turn, was given an interesting briefing on the Medical Center's more recent experiences in organ transplant surgery.

"We've come a long way since Christian Bernhard's pioneering heart transplant experiment, but we definitely are not in the business of performing miracles. Our progress has been difficult to come by, and in more cases than I would care to admit, we have learned from our mistakes.

"We're still in business because there have been numerous successes in organ transplant surgery when no other option remained if the patients were to survive. The improvements in our surgical procedures and the refinements in the selection criteria for matching donor organs to patients are the two most important factors contributing to our increasing successes.

"However, Mr. Coleman, we are always facing the possibility of the patient rejecting the donor organ. We have anti rejection drugs that sometimes can postpone that process indefinitely. What that amounts to is a trade off to save the patient's life by desensitizing his immune system so he has less ability to reject the donor organ while making him less able to fight common viral diseases."

"What about all these reports from the news media announcing major advancements in organ transplant surgery, Doctor? Is the American public being led astray; and is what we are reading in the papers all a hoax? This is what I'm here to find out," Jim was quick to add.

"We are not in the habit of releasing false medical results, Mr. Coleman," said Dr. Armstrong. *Quite the impudent fellow*, he thought. "If you were not on assignment from the Surgeon General's Office, I would terminate this meeting. I have more pressing matters to tend to than to waste time making you into an instant expert." He stood up from his desk, changed his mind, and sat back down. "On second thought, I'll bear with you a bit longer—just to set the record straight." Robert Armstrong was usually not one to lose his composure. Besides, he wanted to find out more about what this guy was up to.

"Please accept my apology, Dr. Armstrong, I didn't mean to appear so abrasive. It's just that I have a job to do, and my goal is to get at the truth."

"Let me answer your questions this way, Jim. Yes, we are experiencing frequent successes every day. However, the fact of the matter is—I cannot tell you why. Sure, our operating room procedures are better, and our candidate selection process has improved, but I can't point my finger at any one significant item that's different today from six months ago.

"We have numerous organ recipients from the past several months who have never required anti rejection drugs; and they are all recovering better than expected with excellent prognoses. This kind of batting average in transplant surgery is unheard of from our prior experiences.

"Frankly, I'm at a loss to explain such a puzzling phenomenon."

"You've just brought to light the purpose for our study, Doctor. Given a large enough number of case histories of those afflicted with hopeless diseases, we are confident that statistical analysis will provide the answers everyone is searching for."

"Well, I'll be honest with you, Jim. In my profession, I cannot rely on statistics when dealing with sick patients. Each is a unique individual, and the details of the surgical procedure he receives are custom to his condition.

"I'm not knocking your area of expertise here, but statistics are a great averaging tool that sometimes will obscure the very information you are seeking. Maybe your study will help to explain away the dilemma that many of us are experiencing. Any honest approach is worth a try at this point.

"In any case, feel free to use whatever information you want from our patient files. Good luck to you and your team."

After Jim's departure, Bob Armstrong reflected on the time spent with him. He had the distinct impression that he was talking with a bureaucrat who was not about to come up with any startling revelations.

While at the Medical Center, Jim found out that a recent heart transplant patient lived in Galveston, close to Houston. A visit with Ben Davidson would certainly help fulfill that contract requirement. After looking up the Davidson number and calling for a short visit, he headed for Galveston.

Arriving at the Davidson home, he saw a healthy-looking man reading the paper on the front porch.

"How do you do, Sir. My name is Jim Coleman. I called a short while ago about seeing a Mr. Davidson."

"I am Ben Davidson, won't you come in? We've been expecting you."

As they shook hands, Mary came out of the kitchen to also greet Jim. "What can we do for you, Mr. Coleman? Mary said something about a survey you are conducting."

"Yes—please, call me Jim—my firm is currently under contract from the Surgeon General's Office to make a worldwide survey of medical patients who are or have been gravely ill from diseases which are usually considered hopeless. Most of our data is to be obtained from large hospitals and medical center files, but we are also required to touch base with patients, like yourself, who are making excellent progress or are in a state of remission.

"Judging from your appearance, Ben, if I may call you by your first name, you certainly look well on the road to a full recovery."

"Yes, and I am grateful to have had the Armstrong team do the retro-fitting of my heart. He is a topnotch heart surgeon in my book."

"I met him earlier today at the Medical Center. He seems like a very busy individual. I just want to ask you a few questions, Ben, and then I'll be on my way."

"Why don't you stay for dinner, Jim? Then you won't be so rushed to find a place to eat," Mary said.

"That's very kind of you, Mary. Why not. I really appreciate your hospitality, Thank you."

"How about a drink before dinner, Jim? Mary and I won't join you because of my own condition —and she just found out today that she's to have a baby—come next February. You are certainly welcome to have a drink of your choice. What's your pleasure, Jim?"

"Thanks, but I'll pass on your offer, I'm not a drinking person. Maybe we can take care of a few of those questions while awaiting dinner, if you don't mind.

"Have you returned to work since your surgery?"

"I sure have. I've been full time at the NASA Space Center since April."

"What kind of work do you do, Ben?"

"I do world demographic studies; actually, I'm head of the section that specializes in developing infrared mapping technology of the Earth's surface."

"That's interesting. Are you on any kind of maintenance medication regimen?"

"None whatsoever—not even anti rejection drugs for my new heart. Doc Armstrong keeps telling me it must have been a perfect match."

"How about physical activity? Do you have any restrictions in the workplace—in your home life?"

Ben burst out laughing at this one. "No—there are none, Jim. Besides, how do you suppose Mary got in the family way?"

Jim turned beet-red from embarrassment and wished he had not asked that last question.

Dinner was served without much conversation generated by Jim. He felt out of place in such a close married couple's household. Any attempt on Ben or Mary's part to draw him out didn't work. Soon after eating, Jim thanked Mary and mumbled something about catching a flight back to Washington.

When he was gone, Mary and her husband had a good laugh about what a strange character the guy was.

10

The data gathering phase of the contract was complete; Luke, Jim and Al reconvened in Washington, DC. The major population centers on the globe had been canvassed, and the database totals edged close to one hundred thousand case histories.

The next contract obligation was to deliver to the Surgeon General's Office a list of case interviews which verified numerous incidents of the total recovery of medical patients diagnosed with incurable illnesses. The list contained 211 names of individuals who were either in a state of remission from their cancers or organ transplant recipients functioning well without anti rejection drugs.

"This ought to keep the Surgeon General's Office from hounding us for a while," Luke gloated with satisfaction as he scanned over the list. "Jim? Let's make sure that enough personal data is included along with the original diagnosis, illness history, treatment, and prognosis.

"Also, structure this preliminary report so that there are two names per page. Present the personal profile in summary form, much like we did during the survey.

"Oh, yes, and compose a cover letter. I'll want to see a draft for my approval before it goes out to final typing."

Luke was definitely taking charge and enjoyed giving orders to his subordinates. On the receiving hand, Jim felt totally crushed by this turn of events. The executive status he had grown accustomed to at CIC was nonexistent. He and Al had been relegated to roles as assistants, and they had no choice in the matter, if they wanted to remain employed.

Two days later, Luke Fieldstone hand-carried twenty-five copies of the report to his contact where it was received with a good amount of enthusiasm.

It took about a week for the Office of the Surgeon General to digest the report's contents, after which time it issued news clips of the recent developments in the field of medicine. The release of information to the press basically confirmed rumors running rampant throughout the world for the past three months that:

MIRACULOUS CURES OF PREVIOUSLY FATAL ILLNESSES ARE ACTUALLY OCCURRING IN THE WORLD.

No claims were made by the medical community that cures were due to recent advances in medicine. Instead, the public was cautioned not to become complacent in their lifestyles and to be thankful that progress was being made in the treatment of previously incurable diseases.

Credit for substantiating this vital information was attributed to a research survey group headed by Dr. Lucas Fieldstone, under contract from the Office of the Surgeon General.

Meanwhile, the team of Fieldstone, Coleman and Steiner implemented the next phase in their study contract: creating the database for statistical analyses. To expedite the process, they hired an outside computer service.

Before correlation testing got underway, Luke called a meeting in his office to instruct Jim and Al about the importance of the task they were embarking on.

"I hope you guys realize that the future of this firm depends on how well you perform to achieve the goals of the contract."

"I don't understand what the hell you're getting at, Luke," Jim interrupted.

"Ditto for me," Al chimed in. "We've done a pretty good job so far—what is it you're so worried about, Luke? Up to now, this organization has looked like a one-man operation, with you getting all the credit."

"Shut up, you little wimp, and listen to me; as far as I'm concerned—you're going to continue making me look good, if we are to remain in business.

"The easy part of this contract is behind us— and we've received all the recognition that we're going to get. Unless we come up with some spectacular discovery in our correlation tests, you can kiss goodbye to any follow-up contract from this government agency."

"You're crying wolf before we've even started the correlation phase, Luke," Jim said. "You know damn well that many government-funded studies are inconclusive, and yet, the very outfits that do these studies keep getting contract after contract for as long as they want to stay in business.

"From past experience, I happen to know that what's important is that we write interesting reports and maintain a good rapport with our contract monitors."

Luke knew Jim was right, but was not about to admit it. He was sitting in the driver's seat, and he had, under his complete control, the best report writer in the industry.

"You take care of your end of the business, Jim, and I'll handle public relations with our customer. In the meantime, get your asses in gear and start correlating."

With the database up and running, the process of massaging the data (in every conceivable way) finally began.

The first parameters to be tested were the most obvious—age and sex of the patients. The computer printouts verified what was already known – serious illness came with age and patients were equally mixed related to gender – but they served as a calibration check of the program algorithm.

Next to be tested: social status; education level; income level; occupation; physical characteristics, like height and weight in comparison to the known averages; family illness history; home location whether urban or rural; geographic latitude (to show possible effects of the sun's radiation); and other parameters of lesser importance.

Jim laughed. "Al, let's dream up as many comparisons as we can; they'll add bulk to the final report."

Unfortunately, none of the tests exhibited a strong correlation with the patient's recovery status or his potential for recovery. "Negative. We can't draw a single meaningful conclusion from this data, any which way," lamented Al.

"Not a problem," said Jim. "I'm already planning to include in the final report recommendations for further study in greater detail."

Luke, however, did not share Jim's attitude. He was feeling squeamish about the lack of anything definitive. *We'll look like failures,* he thought. *This venture will go down the toilet, and unemployment will come to bite us on the ass.* An air of desperation took hold.

"What the hell is the matter with you dummies? Don't you realize we're on the hairy edge of going down the tubes as a business?

"Why can't you apply a little more imagination? The answer has to be somewhere in that large chunk of case data we spent four months gathering," Luke said.

"What else can we do, Luke? You're never around when we could use your great expertise."

This was a far-fetched assessment, since Luke, along with Jim and Al, didn't possess expertise – at least not in the problem-solving department; they'd always relied on (and taken credit for) other people's know-how.

Luke lost it. In his sarcastic manner he blurted out, "HAVE YOU FRIGGIN IDIOTS EVER CONSIDERED COMPARING CHINKS AND NIGGERS WITH WHITE FOLKS?" Then he stormed out.

Without realizing what he'd said, Luke had hit upon an answer.

"I don't know if we should pursue the race factor," Jim said.

"Man, what if he's right? That would solve our problems," Al said.

"But the bastard will have such an inflated ego, it'll be impossible to work for him."

"We don't have any other options if he won't go along with putting recommendations into the report," Al said. "The guy seems desperate.

Maybe he knows something we don't know – it's his contact at the Surgeon General's office."

Jim looked doubtful, but acquiesced. "I guess you're making sense, Al."

Data sorts were run using race as the test parameter. The correlation between the white race and patients on the way to full recovery was so strong, it was almost unbelievable. The discovery caught them completely off guard. Jim and Al didn't know whether to be elated by the sudden turn of events or if they'd be in for another round of abuse from Luke.

They considered the credit to be bestowed upon them as a group, the fame sure to follow, and their assured future success as a study firm. No question about it: they'd take advantage of this golden opportunity.

Their discovery needed to be rock-solid; Jim and Al couldn't afford more ridicule from Luke, so they had to stand on firm ground when they broke the news to him.

In spite of Jim's lack of imagination, he did have the quality of being thorough. Computer printouts were categorized by country, with the total number of patients subdivided into races and further subdivided into survivors within each race.

The results confirmed the earlier racial factor, and the reason for the strong correlation became clearly evident. Countries were populated by a mix of constituent races. The relative number of people comprising each race seemed primarily a function of two important factors: geographical origin and generational ancestry. The computer printout for each country, regardless of the relative concentration of each race making up its population, showed the surviving patients to be White, almost exclusively. An interesting statistic was noted in countries like the US and Russia, where large concentrations of several races received identical levels of medical care, yet only the Whites responded successfully to treatment. There had to be some finite difference in the genetics of the races.

Jim was already thinking of their next contract for a more in-depth study. It should be guaranteed after their spectacular performance on the present contract.

As expected, when Luke was told of the surprising discovery, he was quick to take credit for steering his partners in the right direction. His mood turned around completely, overjoyed at the prospect of worldwide fame. He was also very pleased with the results which seemed to prove his own deep-rooted convictions of White supremacy. His family heritage of plantation life and slave trading included many such prejudices, handed down from generation to generation.

11

Jim knew their final report had to be free of Luke's racial prejudice. And, with amazing self-awareness, he realized that his flair for writing had a tendency to contain egotistical overtones. He'd suppress this air of superiority so as not to jeopardize the favorable position they stood to gain for future contracts. The correlation results were presented graphically to emphasize the thoroughness of their effort. The absence of correlation in most of the tests served to reinforce the single, strong racial correlation: definite proof of positive White reaction to modern medical science. Individual case histories were cited to emphasize the favorable turnaround of White patients after receiving treatment.

After minor editorial comment from Luke (he was not about to expose his lack of writing skills), the report was approved for printing. The required 25 copies once again delivered to the Surgeon General's Office.

The reaction at the Surgeon General's office was one of incredulity. No one would have suspected there could be a racial factor connected with the miraculous recoveries of doomed patients occurring with increasing frequency all over the world. Could it be that the results were in error because of the chance happening that only Whites had reacted positively? Certainly the database was large enough, and statistics don't usually lie. Yet, wasn't there the remote possibility that significantly more Whites than nonwhites reacted favorably to treatment because there were so many more Whites treated in the first place.

After careful consideration, weighing the pros and cons of how to handle such a development, the Surgeon General's Office chose to be candid with the American public. The news couldn't be kept secret; it was only a matter of time before it became obvious. Who knew how the various races in the world would react? Misinterpretation of facts could lead to chaos and even a revival of open warfare between races.

A single criticism of the report related to its statistical methods for obtaining information. Even though the results were presented objectively and without intended bias, the missing attempt to explain what the reason might be for them left many unanswered questions and showed a lack of sensitivity.

It was decided that the best way to go public was to have a press conference. Honesty and openness had always been the best way to avoid misinterpretation down the line. The agency would stress the prospect of longer life expectancy as a benefit for all of mankind, regardless of race, and hopefully create an air of optimism among the world populace.

It did not take long before the press corps issued its own analysis of the findings. The "think tank" group headed by Dr. Lucas Fieldstone received notoriety from the news media. Television interviews on major talk shows contributed to the worldwide fame bestowed upon them. Luke was delighted with the credit he received as leader of the group. His head swam fantasizing about speaking invitations sure to come and spectacular words of wisdom he would conjure up.

A subject as important as new medical technology for the treatment of fatal diseases was exactly what the news media liked to get involved with. It didn't waste time coming up with its own interpretation of the noteworthy events. Possible explanations, as well as consequences, were discussed in great detail on radio and television panels, newspaper editorials, and magazine feature articles.

Frequently, however, the press's non-definitive methods left the audience in a quandary as to what was actually true. When possible variations of a subject were presented, it made for interesting listening or reading as a form of entertainment, but final conclusions or interpretation of what was factual fell to each individual whose attention had been aroused.

The net result of these lengthy yet inconclusive commentaries was that racial groups the world over were left in a state of uncertainty. Members of the White race, although initially stunned, could not help but feel enormous relief if they no longer had to fear an untimely death preceded by pain and suffering. Small-minded Whites, those still mired in bigotry, felt vindicated – their rightful destiny to inherit the Earth finally evident. By contrast, people of nonwhite races suddenly shared a glaring problem – the blatant inequity related to medical care and health. *Every single race* other than White would continue to endure the agony of terminal illness? For eons there had been statistics linking those living in poverty (disproportionately people of color), and mortality rates, but this was a new level of injustice altogether.

While most nonwhites remained calm, clinging to the hope that this development could benefit them as well, a simmering resentment of Whites by certain groups gradually approached the boiling point. Ingredients were present to instigate tumultuous racial unrest, (even revenge against Whites, for the most radical of the disenfranchised); all that remained necessary was a suitable trigger to start the process,

The stage had been set, not only to alienate Whites from the rest of the human race, but also to punish them for their perceived historically selfish actions.

12

JULY

While the Fieldstone study contract neared completion and the final report was being written, the six-month chemotherapy test period on terminal cancer patients came to an end.

The auditorium at the Gerber Clinic filled up with patients who had participated in the test program. Their physical appearance ranged from those who were very sick to a goodly number who didn't seem to have any type of ailment.

Promptly at nine o'clock, Dr. Stevens stood at the podium to welcome the group back to Gerber. After a few words of appreciation for their patience and cooperation, he turned the meeting over to Dr. Arnold Goldman who had presided at the last meeting back in January.

"First of all, I want to thank every one of you who persevered with us through this very trying period. Your participation in this test may lead us to better understanding of cancer in its forms in future years. We at Gerber are hopeful that the treatment you have undergone will provide us with necessary techniques to evaluate responses to therapy. Not all of you were able to make it back for our meeting, and that is understandable. Six months ago you were all extremely sick people. I'm sure a number of you did not expect to be with us on this date. For the record, 69 original test members are not here, 43 have passed away, and 26 are too ill to attend.

"Please forgive me for appearing so "matter-of-factly" when referring to your physical well-being. I don't mean to appear unsympathetic; it's just that in this business we have not enjoyed too many successes, and our expectations have fallen short too frequently.

"Now, let's look at the positive. Seeing you as a group, from where I stand, I would venture to guess that a number of you are in better condition now than when we started six months ago. Certainly, I can guess that you are not worse off than when the tests started.

Participants and their family members also eyed the group. Those who were obviously ill craned their necks, clearly assessing as many other patients as they could. Who was as sick as they? Who looked to be in recovery?

Molly shifted in her seat, her glowing skin a magnet for sorrowful and suspicious looks. *Why should I feel ashamed to be better? I could just as easily have been given a placebo.* Survivor guilt was a tough cross to bear in a group such as this.

"Our next task is to appraise your physical condition to find out the extent of progress. We'd like to keep you here for the rest of the day and most of tomorrow for a complete screening which will consist of a thorough examination and clinical tests. Then, we ask that you return to your homes and await word of your evaluation. Please stay where you are until your name is called. Our medical staff will take over from there. Thank you all for coming."

"Doctor!" A woman was on her feet, and Dr. Goldman turned back to the podium. "My husband's condition…it's worse." She put her hand on the shoulder of the man sitting next to her. Though ashen, his dark complexion was obvious. "I'm looking around the room and seeing that some people don't even look like they're sick anymore. You should give everybody the medicine! It must work!"

"Yeah," a couple others echoed.

"I don't want to die for science if I don't have to," squeaked a woman a couple rows down from Molly.

Dr. Goldman's mouth tensed, his face seemed to redden. "Your feelings are understandable," he said, "but this is a scientific study – all of you knew this could be the outcome when you signed up. I'm sorry…"

The woman would not sit down, "Is it because we're Black? I've watched the programs. Is anyone of color in this room in recovery?" she asked, scanning the auditorium.

At first it appeared that her accusation would bear fruit, but then a man in the third row, raised his arm. "I am African American," he said, rising and turning around. "And my health has improved."

Dr. Stevens quickly moved towards the microphone. "Ladies and Gentlemen, we know this is difficult, heartbreaking, but we must continue our evaluations. There are numerous factors which will impact remission, Madam. Statistically speaking, there are frequently a small number of patients who improve even on the placebo. I hear your distress, and I'd like you and your husband to meet with staff on our team. One of the nurses will escort you to the office."

The woman, making not the slightest effort to wipe away the tears rolling down her cheeks, allowed herself and her husband to be led from the room. Molly and Tom exchanged looks, their hearts going out to the couple. That could have been them. Molly felt grateful to be one of the first called for her examination. The attending nurse escorted her to the office of Dr. Johnston, her physician since she first visited Gerber.

"You are a healthy looking, young specimen, Molly. Where did you get such a nice tan?" Dr. Johnston could not help but notice it as he examined Molly.

"Oh, this was a part of my therapy prescribed by my husband. We spent a week in Cancun during the later part of May," Molly answered with a twinkle in her eyes.

"It did you no harm, Molly. And isn't this a coincidence? My wife and I have been there a few times and enjoyed our trip so much that we bought two weeks of a timeshare at a place called Clipper Club. There is a wide variety of activities to take part in at a place like Cancun as I'm sure you and your husband already know.

"Now, getting back to business at hand. You appear to be making a remarkable recovery. Your records show that you are in remission. If I didn't know better, you are a different person than when I last saw you back in January. How do you feel in general?"

"Well, I'll share a secret with you. If my husband and family had not been so supportive, I don't think I would be here today.

"My withdrawal from morphine was the worst nightmare of my life. Tom was so patient; he made sure I had the best care possible and that I maintained my daily dose of chemo – even when I had trouble holding the pills down."

"Do you feel the chemo is the reason for your recovery?"

"I don't know, but I like to believe it is. Tom has spent a good part of his life at medical institutions, and he has never seen such a quick turnabout from a hopeless case like mine."

"Of course, I can't tell you at this point if you actually received the chemotherapy, as that is still under wraps. My guess is that you were administered the real stuff, Molly."

"So, Doc, do you think I'll make it?"

"I'd say your chances are very good. I am about finished with the exam, and I must tell you that your vital signs are excellent. Your lung region sounds very normal, and your EKG tells me your heart action is perfect.

"Don't forget your lab tests first thing tomorrow morning. You are scheduled for blood work and x-rays; tissue samples will be taken from your chest area for analysis at the pathology lab. Good luck to you, Molly, and say hello to Tom for me, will you?"

Molly thanked Dr. Johnson, then dressed.

While Molly was being examined, Tom met with Dr. Stevens to discuss details of the test program.

"Now that the test period is over, Dr. Stevens, what are your first impressions about the progress of some of your patients?" Tom couldn't hold back from asking, even though he knew it was premature, certainly until all the facts were in. After seeing his own Molly go from a hopeless condition six months ago to practically a new person today, he couldn't help but wonder what was so different in her treatment— this time around.

"I'm not surprised you are inquisitive, Tom, after what you and Molly have been through. When I saw the large number of these patients at the meeting who are pictures of health—including Molly, I too, am dumbfounded. It's almost unbelievable! I have been in this business for a good many years, and never have I seen such a positive response to a new therapy for the treatment of cancer."

"I know," replied Tom. "The last biopsy we did on Molly showed perfectly normal tissue patterns— like there had never been any cancerous cells in the first place. Dead cells usually leave a trail – somewhat like scar tissue, but none of those signs were present as early as two months ago."

"I'll tell you what, Tom, it certainly looks like we have stumbled onto something which may well revolutionize the treatment of cancer in the years to come.

"I'm sure you realize, however, that we at Gerber are only a test center for new pharmaceuticals. The best we can hope for are positive patient reactions, and then maybe we can devise an intelligent method of quantifying the magnitude of progress— when there is any."

"That's putting it in a candid way, Doc. You can't draw conclusions too early in this game. It's like an election; the winner is not known for sure until all the returns are in."

"That's right, Tom. After these screening tests, we should have a much better idea how effective this new chemotherapy really is."

"How much longer will it be, before you're ready to announce the results?"

"You'd better give us a week before expecting to hear from us. Heck, at this point we don't even know who is paired with whom. And then, which one in each pair got the real treatment?

"I bet we're in for some startling revelations. Wouldn't you say, Tom?"

"Yes, I'm sure you and your staff are in for some interesting sessions. Molly must be wondering where I disappeared to, so I had better head back to the auditorium.

"Thanks for your time, Dr. Stevens. I wish you success on a very challenging program. Molly and I will be anxious to hear from you."

The two men of medical science, although with different specialties, had a parting handshake, each knowing that new frontiers in medicine were about to emerge. Tom knew it would have been indelicate to even ask about the racial component. Besides, there was that man who was making progress, who had stood up. Tom was eager to learn the results.

It took a total of three days to complete the screening of all patients who had made it to the meeting. The next step was to obtain a printout of the pairing information and the chemo assignment.

Dr. Stevens addressed the Gerber staff members involved in the latest testing procedure. "Esteemed colleagues, we are about to find out if the method to our madness will finally have a payoff." The printer hummed behind him. "At this point I'd like Arnold Goldman to take over because this whole experiment was his from the beginning. Why don't you go ahead, Arnie?"

"Thank you, Erik. The printout generating is from the first stage of the program six months ago. We'll get our first glimpse at how our test group was paired off and how the chemotherapy was assigned. Here it comes!"

The staff members seemed to sit up straighter in anticipation. Anecdotally, it was obvious that the medication had been effective; in a few more moments they'd have the hard data to back up that assertion. It escaped no one that a good amount of reliance and trust had been put on the computer program to select identical pairs and play God and choose the recipient for the new drug.

The printed information came out neatly formatted in a listing of 113 pairs of names with the appropriate asterisk. Everyone present had a keen interest in finding out where his own patients appeared on the list, who their partners were, and not the least of all – were they receiving chemotherapy?

SOMETHING HAD GONE AWRY!! At first glance, several of the patients who were known to be in remission were listed as not receiving chemo.

Molly Curtis, for one, did not receive any chemo, according to the printout.

"Goddammit! I knew right from the start that we shouldn't have put so much faith in a simple-minded computer! What do we do now?" one of the skeptics in the group bellowed.

"Come now. Let's not lose our cool. You can't pass judgment till all the facts are in. How about continuing with the remaining printouts?" someone else interjected.

There were quite a few confused and disappointed individuals in the room.

The printed listing from the next program stage integrated the screening results in summary form next to each name.

This one confirmed what had already been noticed on the first listing. Many recovering patients never received chemotherapy. Even more surprising, many who had received it were not faring well at all. Molly's twin patient had passed away on the 17th of May.

The last listing from the third program stage was generated strictly as an exercise, because no one was placing much faith in its content at that point. The program to produce this listing was supposed to quantify the progress in each pair once the benchmark from the placebo recipient was factored in.

The printout made no sense. Negative process showed up in over half of the pairs.

"It appears that we have one screwed up mess on our hands," Arnie Goldman said.

"Why don't we call it quits for tonight because we're getting nowhere fast at this point in time," he continued. "There has to be a logical explanation— and we'll find it— we're just not thinking straight right now— we'd better sleep on it."

Needless to say, Arnold Goldman felt totally disheartened at this unexpected turnaround. He stayed behind to take a closer look at the printouts.

In the morning, Arnold Goldman met with Erik Stevens to decide how to handle the unpredictable results. The experiment was either a total failure or, there had been a slip up somewhere in the planning of its actual execution.

"This is the tally of our results so far, Erik. Of the 226 participants, 43 passed away as of three days ago, another 26 are not expected to live longer than a few more weeks, 53 have shown measurable improvement and their vital signs are good. The remaining 104 are making excellent progress— some even look like they'd never had this dreaded disease.

"Here is the kicker. Of the recovering group of 104, only 21 were on chemo."

"The question is— what do we do next, Arnie? We certainly can't make any of this public— not until we get some answers, anyway."

"Here's what I'd like to do," Arnie replied. "I don't believe our experiment is at fault. Something else is going on that we are not aware of. We've read in newspapers for the last couple of months about these miraculous recoveries of ill people with deadly diseases— on a daily basis. I'm thinking there has to be a connection. I say we keep this whole project under wraps until we know more about what's going on."

"I agree with you, Arnie, there isn't much else we can do right now. Why don't you have staff call the participants and tell them the results are encouraging but inconclusive. Thank them for their cooperation. Tell them also to use up the remainder of their pills and we will be in touch shortly.

"In the meantime, we'll contact the Office of the Surgeon General to find out what the hell is going on. That visit with Jim Coleman didn't tell us much."

"Erik, do you think we should crunch the data, using race as the correlation factor?"

"Jeez, Arnie, what a stretch. Some of the latest science doesn't even recognize different races, one –homo sapien – ethnic characteristics are seen as superficial."

"Controversy, just what we don't need. Sandra Gillman, in infectious diseases, has spent decades studying racially-specific illness. Let's get a consult with her – if, the Surgeon General's Office sees this as a trend. And this might be a whim, but between me and you – yes, crunch the data."

13

The accolades bestowed on the Fieldstone team, as it was now called, appeared to be short lived. Barely three weeks after the press conference at the Surgeon General's Office, followed by widespread publicity, the drop-off in public interest signaled to the press that top billing in the news was no longer justified. Any write-ups for magazine and newspaper trades were relegated to filler material. Likewise, radio and television programming almost completely stopped referencing the study.

Perhaps the Fieldstone Study was being superseded by reports of a dramatic decrease in the number of new cancers and rates of highly successful organ transplants. The Surgeon General's Office reeled in their promotion of the study. Murmurs circulated of an as yet unknown phenomenon was causing the sudden improvement in the well-being of White citizenry world-wide.

The awarding of a follow-up contract to the Fieldstone team was delayed. After all, Luke Fieldstone and his partners had been well paid for uncovering the racial factor as it applied to serious disease and treatment response. However, it appeared that patient recovery had nothing to do with the kind of treatment received. Patients were destined to recover because cancer itself was on the way out among Whites. Furthermore, it was possible that organ transplant surgery had become successful on the same racial group because the rejection mechanism to fight off the transplant was no longer in evidence.

Something strange was happening in the world, and the scientific community was slowly coming around to that realization. Answers seemed to point to White genetic makeup.

For his part, Luke Fieldstone wasn't ready to give up the limelight. Fame and fortune might be fleeting, but it wasn't going to disappear *that* fast. A spectacular revelation – that's what he'd have to come up with if he and his team were to regain public esteem.

The recent invitation to speak at the World Congress on Population Trends in Geneva, Switzerland, would be the logical place to reclaim their due credits. The meeting was two weeks away. Luke had to notify his partners posthaste.

"I hope you guys realize our little corporation is on the verge of going down the tubes unless we can come up with a real scoop to put us back in the headlines. That follow-up contract is not coming any time soon. Do either one of you have any ideas to put us back in business?"

Luke didn't expect any suggestions; he knew Jim and Al weren't the most imaginative people around. Sure enough, their faces looked pretty blank. No problem, he'd use the opportunity to advance his own agenda.

"All right. I will be presenting my talk at the Geneva conference in a couple of weeks, and my plan is to announce that recent world developments, as evidenced by our own study, indicate superior traits in the White component of the human race."

"Luke, are you out of your mind?" Jim asked.

"Now simmer down, Jim. You know damn well that the study data showed Whites to be superior— so what's the point in hiding it?

"We have tons of documentation to prove it, and newspaper accounts of the disappearance of cancer among Whites tells us that we are destined to be around for a long time to come.

"If we are to capitalize on these events, we have to be at the forefront with our own claims before they become an established fact. Don't you agree that my plan makes sense?

"Can you imagine the paid speaking engagements this could generate? Hell, we could go on tour, make big bucks and get all kinds of publicity.

"All we need is a prepared talk that each one of us could use on the tour, along with a set of appropriate slides and we're in business – like a traveling road show.

"Think of the possibilities, Jim. We can have it made in the shade."

"Much as I hate to admit it, you may be right, Luke, but that's a taboo subject in modern society. When I wrote the final report on our study program, I went out of my way to avoid the mention of White supremacy. Now you want to blow the lid off and who knows what reactions that could trigger. I'm sorry, but I can't go along with you."

"Listen to me— you're being chicken. When opportunity knocks, you're supposed to run with it.

"Have I given you guys any bum steers since we went into business? I'm the one who proposed the study program in the first place. Then, when you were hung up interpreting the data, I pointed you in the right direction by bringing up the racial factor.

"Come on. You know damned well I'm right. Don't you have the courage of your convictions?"

Not surprisingly, Jim and Al didn't have ideas of their own to offer as alternatives to Luke's proposal. The future of their study group boiled down to one of two choices. Either they dissolved their partnership by going out of business, or they could go along with Luke on the chance that he'd open up new sources of income for them.

Luke was a convincing salesman. How could they turn him down? They'd done alright by him so far — why not go along with him?

"OK." Jim looked at his yes-man, Al, who of course nodded in agreement. "You talked us into it, Luke. Where do we start?"

"First off…I'd like you, Jim, to compose a thirty-minute talk. I want lots of slides to show how the survey data was tested to establish correlation with every parameter used during the analytical phase of the study program.

"Then bring out the racial test and make sure to stress the strong correlation of Whites responding favorably to the latest medical advances.

"The next part of the talk should supplement our findings with the most recent reports of the decrease in the incidence of cancer among Whites."

At this point Al interrupted. "Wait just a minute, Luke. If some unknown factor is making the White race healthier than the remaining races in the world, how do we know if the latest medical advances were the reason for these sudden recoveries?"

"That's a surprisingly good point, Al, but it's not important when we consider the end result. What the hell do we care how it happened? The fact is that Whites are faring better than all other races.

"The concluding remarks should be a declaration that the White race is the superior race on Earth. The data from our survey and recent developments in the world are proof positive that this is the one and only logical conclusion. You've got two weeks to pull it together."

Luke's paper was not scheduled till the afternoon of the second day of the World Congress on Population Trends, but he decided to attend all of the sessions anyway.

The presentation of papers got underway shortly after the keynote address by the world-renowned heart surgeon, Dr. Robert Armstrong, from the Houston Medical Center. The thrust of his talk was on the future wellbeing of the human race. Longer life spans were expected as well as an increasing population which, aided by the greater mobility of the times, would redistribute itself in closer proximity to natural resources.

Dr. Armstrong received a lively round of applause for a speech right on target.

Luke listened to presentations during the first day's sessions on subjects ranging from medicine to scientific developments to population increases in emerging third world countries.

The talk that Luke found most compelling was on the subject of demography. The paper dealt primarily with infrared monitoring of the

Earth's surface to detect mass migrations of people to different areas on the globe. Luke was interested for a different reason. The presenter was Benjamin Davidson from NASA, who he recognized right away as one of the patients interviewed during their survey.

After the session Luke hung back to meet him.

"You chose a very appropriate topic for a meeting such as this, Mr. Davidson. The subject matter is fascinating, and I'm sure this application of narrow band infrared techniques to the science of demography will be useful in future years."

"Well, thank you, Mr. Fieldstone. For your information, we already have a prototype system in operation that may have you under surveillance right this minute. Big brother may be watching you," Ben said, grinning.

"I have a second reason for wanting to meet you, Ben. Aren't you the heart transplant recipient we interviewed during our recent survey for the Surgeon General's Office?"

"If you are referring to the visit my wife and I had with a fellow named Coleman—I think it was; yes, I'm the guy. That guy, Coleman, as I recall sure was a strange character."

"He happens to work for me; and I agree he can come off a bit odd, but he is a good worker." Luke knew all too well that he couldn't get along without Jim under the present set of circumstances.

"You look like a picture of health, I must say. Do you feel like you are fully recovered from the transplant operation?"

"I sure do. Besides, if I run into trouble, my doctor is right here at the meeting. Did you hear Dr. Armstrong earlier? Well, he's the one who operated on me.

"Incidentally, are you also presenting a paper at this meeting?"

"Yes. I'm scheduled for tomorrow afternoon. I'll be talking about cases like your own— and principally, cancer patients— and how they are doing so well. We may put your infrared gear to the test very shortly when the Western World has its population explosion."

"Unfortunately, Dr. Armstrong and I are scheduled to head back to Houston this afternoon, so we'll miss your talk. But best of luck with it," Ben said.

"Oh, that's unfortunate; it promises to be a highlight of the conference," said Luke. And with that, they parted company.

Luke's talk caused quite an uproar. Many attendees, regardless of race, walked out of the auditorium in protest before the customary question and answer period. There was no doubt that serious repercussions would follow.

The conference leaders could have averted the controversy if Luke had gone through formal channels to get his paper approved; it would surely have been rejected. Since he was late submitting the draft, the review committee had no time to pass judgment. They green-lighted it; after all, a paper from the Surgeon General's Office survey team?

Without realizing the implications, Luke's claim of White supremacy and the widely accepted data he used to prove his argument, just about wiped out any gains humankind had made over the past decades to do away with racial prejudice.

Luke himself was such a bigoted individual, that in his own mind all he had done was bring out the truth about the superiority of the White race. The bad press that he and his partners garnered in response to his *faux pas* was nothing compared to societal damage set in motion.

In one respect, the bad name the Fieldstone team brought upon itself severed any possibility of future business with the US government. Medical institutions throughout the country raised objections to the federal government wasting money supporting such misleading studies. The Gerber Cancer Clinic and the Houston Medical Center were only two of many groups that participated in these protests.

On the other hand, even though Luke's plan backfired, the subject matter generated a considerable amount of interest with racist organizations throughout the Western World. In particular, Ku Klux Klan groups, splinter groups which constantly attempted a revival of Nazism, and White racists from South Africa were very interested in paying for guest lectures. Then there were numerous institutions of higher learning in both the US and Europe whose student organizations naively requested guest appearances, offering sizable fees.

The Fieldstone team embarked on a business mission quite different from its original charter of doing "think tank" studies. Well paid for their efforts (in spite of the adverse publicity), each approached his new task as if a pioneer advancing the cause of mankind. So what if it was slanted highly in favor of the White race? The notoriety obtained went a long way towards satisfying their thirst for fame, even if the label of racist was attached to it.

On September 29th, one month since the completion of their contract with the Office of the Surgeon General. The team of Fieldstone, Coleman and Steiner moved into a new phase on its path to achieve infamy. Luke had done the biggest selling job of his career when he talked Jim into following him. Jim realized he'd committed a blunder when he agreed to go along, but figured it was too late to turn back, now that they were barred from any future study contracts with the government. As for Al, he didn't have the backbone or drive to make a decision on his own. Subordinate to Jim for many years he would follow him anywhere as the obedient crony without ever questioning his motives. Luke wielded complete control of them, but the moral outrage was starting to have an effect on Jim. Even though monetary compensation was more than adequate, Jim had the uneasy feeling that they were tampering with the destiny of mankind.

By contrast, Luke enjoyed his role as the bearer of good tidings to members of the White race concerning their racial superiority. Every speech was delivered with greater intensity, and the message was galvanized into one to unify Whites in preparation to inherit the Earth.

The trigger had been pulled: racial extremists were emboldened, and the bullet of hostility would seek its mark. Luke and his timid cohorts managed to accomplish the feat – simply to satisfy their own selfish motives.

14

OCTOBER

At first, public reaction to the Fieldstone claims of White supremacy was one of utter amazement – how could statistics back up prejudice, long thought to be an emotionally taught, ignorant perspective? The slow progression of civilized society, interspersed with eras of oppression by all races, had reached its present level where equality of all human beings was accepted by the majority, the world over. The waging of a racial war had become unthinkable. The insanity of this latest revelation seemed like an attempt to drive a wedge between the races. Most Whites, as well as nonwhites, appeared united in a common cause to prevent this separation from taking place and to avoid violence at all cost.

Continuing scientific reports, however, served as a constant reminder that Whites seemed to be more resistant to genetically-related diseases. New cancers among Whites either were not being reported or they didn't occur. The question begging an answer: Was the protection of the White race due to an intentional mechanism? Was a deliberate "racial cleansing" being initiated, and if so, by whom? Suspicion and paranoia fed a growing undercurrent of resentment and anger towards this privileged status.

On the other side of the spectrum, bigotry buried for years, erupted like a volcano forever under pressure. White supremacists used widespread news coverage of the Fieldstone claim as propaganda to further their cause. The Ku Klux Klan resumed the use of the burning cross as their trademark and the wearing of white-hooded robes at meetings. The gatherings were no longer clandestine as in the old days. They boldly congregated openly in order to get as much publicity as possible. The spread of the Klan was like a cancer; meetings of hate multiplied over the Western Hemisphere. Neo-Nazi groups returned across Western Europe.

Even though a large majority of the White population opposed the outbursts of racism, it was powerless to do anything to curb them within existing laws guaranteeing freedom of speech and the press. Historically, insane radicals had almost never been stopped in time to prevent harm to society – events happened too rapidly for the democratic process to be effective. An unpreventable confrontation between humans who felt fearful and unjustly treated, and those who felt most empowered was birthed – each desperate to ensure their survival.

However, the escalating tempo of racist demonstrations backfired. Meetings were infiltrated in growing numbers by nonwhites in an attempt to quell their effectiveness. So far the interference has been peaceful except for a few isolated cases of fights between individuals, and these were quickly broken up. Yet despite these non-violent encounters, a rising tide of dislike for Whites rose, and many found themselves on the defensive.

Within the short timespan of less than one month since Luke Field-stone delivered his paper at the World Congress on Population Trends, nonwhites using social media inflamed the situation and fed the fires of hatred for the White race, and white supremacists acted in kind. Although there was no way to predict where it would strike, violence felt imminent.

The Ku Klux Klan made the first mistake during the night of October 19th, in a bold move to demonstrate its right of authority. In the small town of Magnolia, Mississippi, a Black male and an immigrant Vietnamese female teenager were stripped naked and hung from a tree limb near the town hall. In a gesture to leave no doubt about who was responsible, a burning cross blazed on site.

A subversive war had begun, and the ugliness of retaliation was on its way.

15

Two days after the Magnolia incident, a bizarre response signaled the beginning of a period of terror experienced by many Whites. For some nonwhites, a primitive, uncontrollable monster had been roused from dormancy to engage in a fight for survival. Its first task was to inflict revenge on members of the White race for past, and expected forthcoming, atrocities. The message blared – loud and clear – if the White component of the human race had any thoughts about being the privileged class, destined to inherit the Earth, they had better revise their thinking; their numbers would not be allowed to multiply.

During the night of October 21st, fifteen Klansmen, who had participated in the cruel murders barely two days before, were secretly rounded up at the farmhouse of one of the Klan members while the rest of the household slept. Each one was gagged, stripped naked, and bound. All of them were taken to an isolated grove of trees located about 200 yards behind the barn, and hung from separate tree limbs.

The following morning, dogs barking at the scene of the mass execution drew the attention of the townspeople to a horrible discovery. Off to the side of the dangling victims, white robes and hoods were heaped in a neat pile. Causing some witnesses to gag, the most gruesome detail of the tableau was the pile of their castrated genitals close to the KKK garments. The significance seemed obvious — a warning to members of supremacy groups – the White race would not be permitted to become the sole heirs of the planet.

Reporters and television personnel descended upon the town of Magnolia like vultures out to claim their version of the sensational developments. Never during the history of this small southern town had it ever experienced such notoriety.

The incidents of the last two days were obviously related, and the role of the Klan unquestioned, but not one clue was found to help identify the responsible party for the second barbarous act. There was no doubt it was retaliation for the senseless murders of two innocent persons. The fact that the victims were of different ethnicities created uncertainty about the perpetrator – or could it have been a team effort?

The story made headlines over the next few days, but further information was not forthcoming – on any angle. Reference was made to an adage right out of the bible: the principle of an eye for an eye and a tooth for a tooth, a convincing deterrent for anyone contemplating a crime against his fellowman.

The sentiment of some White Americans was that the Ku Klux Klan received exactly what it deserved. After all, the Klan committed a crime, which provoked an equally aggressive response. The method of repayment, although undeniably harsh, could have been expected. Others were appalled at the escalation of violence in the small town and concerned that the guilty parties were unidentifiable. Most regarded the incidents as a local flare-up of racial bigotry that got out of hand. It was an anomaly, a temporary loss of common decency that never should have happened, and it would be best to forget it ever took place. A return to normalcy was sure to follow; in civilized society, there was no place for crimes of prejudice.

As it turned out, the Magnolia Massacre was the forerunner of numerous, similar incidents designed to intimidate Whites – the perceived threat to all other races.

One week later, October 27th, on a remote beach south of San Diego, near the Mexican border, five White males washed ashore – apparently drowning victims. When the beach patrol was alerted and retrieved the bodies (also naked), it was obvious their genitals were missing. Upon further examination, drowning was quickly ruled out when each victim was found to have a bullet hole in their head. The time spent in the water had been long enough to wash off blood flow from the wound, so initially, the bullet's entry point wasn't visible.

"Gang slaying on a small boat, like a fishing boat, maybe a few miles offshore to avoid detection?" said one of the lifeguards.

"Then the bodies were dumped overboard near the beach to wash ashore," said another.

"But this…you know…" The chief lifeguard pointed at where their genitals should have been. "Weird. I'll make the call to the police."

Within ten minutes, a police cruiser followed by an ambulance pulled up.

"Let's get the crowd away from here before things get out of hand or someone panics," an officer said, approaching the scene.

The beach patrolmen quickly roped off an out-of-bounds section to keep spectators back.

"This is one hell-of-a-way to castrate someone," remarked the detective. "They cut off the whole apparatus— like they were trying to turn them into chicks."

He eyed the scene. "Not much more we can do here, fellas, so let's load the bodies into the ambulance for the ride back to headquarters, and the police docs will have a look at them. We can probably get some ID's through fingerprints to notify next of kin. This might also give us a clue into their backgrounds and why somebody would be so knife happy."

"For their sake, I hope these guys weren't alive when this butchering job was done," commented one of the lifeguards, watching as they wrapped the bodies in blankets and placed them in the ambulance.

Autopsies confirmed death by gunshot to the head, no longer than 12 hours earlier. Probably just luck that they weren't found by sharks before washing ashore. Castration had been performed a few hours later as evidenced by an absence of bleeding, due to prior clotting in the blood vessels adjoining the open wounds. Why would anyone perform such a heinous act, unless it was intended to convey some sort of message?

Fingerprints identified three of the victims as native Californians from White middle-class families living in the Santa Barbara region.

Further checking revealed that they were honor students at the local university at Santa Barbara.

The university confirmed that five of its White, male students had been absent from classes that morning. The bodies proved to be those of the missing students. All five were clean-living, young men, going about the business of getting an education. Their social life on campus was considered normal with no evidence of addiction to alcohol or drugs that might provide a lead worth investigating.

Not one shred of evidence could steer homicide in a logical direction for an investigation.

Later that same morning, a newsflash from San Francisco told of the discovery of four White, male bodies on a remote beach off Highway 1 in the town of Pacifica. The bodies had been brutally decapitated and also castrated. A short time later, the missing heads and mangled genitals were located next to a trash barrel in a black, plastic garbage bag, nearby.

It didn't seem like a crime of passion – more like a vendetta for some unknown reason. The victims, after identification from fingerprints, were found to be individuals with normal backgrounds and honorable credentials that provided no leads as to a possible motive for such a barbaric act.

A day later in Central Park North, New York City, six more bodies were uncovered under a pile of leaves by a group of joggers who happened to notice bloody spots on the dry leaves as they ran by. All White males, their trousers were saturated with blood from the crude ritual of castration. From the profuse amount of bleeding, it remained questionable whether the victims died as a direct result of being cut up so badly – or from a gunshot to the head. Impossible to know if the executioners had shown mercy. Again, there was no obvious motive why upstanding citizens should be so brutally massacred.

Meanwhile, the FBI had been brought into the picture. Similar incidents were taking place, practically on a daily basis, at seemingly random locations all over the country. Even in Hawaii and Alaska, reports told of similar crimes against White males— and no clues as to the responsible parties. The bureau futilely tried to establish a pattern to help identify the motive. Methodical in its investigations and not prone to make snap judgments that could backfire, the FBI considered everything. It seemed likely that the murders were racially-based. In fact, it was even possible that a White terrorist group was behind the entire matter – in an attempt to incite a racial war. Likewise, there was no way to know, with certainty, that the terrorist acts were those of organized nonwhites. So far, there hadn't been acts of violence so numerous that calling it an all-out war against the White race was justified.

As their starting point, the Bureau reviewed events of the last nine months. The sequence of assumed circumstances produced a worst-case scenario, which painted a very bleak picture of civilized society. Was it possible that mankind was about to self-destruct in a war of survival, possibly caused by a misinterpretation of a few out of the ordinary recent events? Citing lack of evidence, the FBI decided to stall for more time, to see if the provocations would come to a stop or if a pattern would emerge which might help to identify who was behind it all.

Meanwhile, contact with Interpol, the international equivalent of the FBI, was made to find out if similar acts of terrorism had been taking place in the rest of the world. The replies from bureaus in Europe confirmed the worst fears imaginable. Yes— brutal crimes were being committed against White people on a daily basis and for no apparent reason.

The first reported crime had taken place during the night of October 22nd, in the Chinese section of London. Early in the evening, seven members of a visiting soccer team from Germany had gone to a Chinese restaurant. Their bodies were discovered that same night in a back ally by a policeman doing rounds on his night beat.

All seven had been stabbed several times in the chest area, which was later established as the cause of death. Further examination of the bodies revealed that each had been castrated, genitals removed. The significance of this act of brutality was not immediately apparent, but believed to be a retaliation for possibly a sex-related crime. Scotland Yard had been on the case, but so far had not uncovered meaningful clues as to suspects or motive for such a sinister crime.

The very next day, a group of vacationers on a weekend tourism trip to the Greek Islands were reported missing when they failed to return to their resort hotel that night. The next morning, bodies of five males in the group were found in a flat area at the summit of a rocky hill on a nearby island. There they were, staked to the ground, face up, as if on a sacrificial altar being offered up to the Gods. The bodies were unclad and looked like they had been tortured and beaten to death, judging by the multiple stabbings and bruises on each one. Most obvious on the bodies were the missing genitals. These had been carved out and were found in a pile off to one side.

The females in the group had been missing ever since the bodies of their male companions were discovered. It was presumed that they, too, had been brutally murdered and their remains not yet found.

Local authorities were investigating, and there had been no break in the case.

Whoever was responsible for these cruel and inhumane acts was doing a masterful job of covering their tracks, because no clues were to be found.

Surprisingly, the Soviet Union reported a case two days later of an ambush of one of their military reconnaissance patrols from a remote outpost near the Indian border. All members of the White Russian Calvary unit, who were expert horsemen, apparently rode into a trap, where they were caught by surprise and never had a chance to defend themselves. Later, a search party discovered that the entire unit had been slaughtered by a barrage of poison blow darts, such as were used by warriors in the Incan empire in South America. This type of weaponry had never been seen outside of the wilds of that continent except possibly in the most remote parts of Africa.

The only wounds found on the victims' bodies were the punctures by darts at random points of impact indicating a surprise attack. Darts were still lodged in the skin of many of the corpses. Later examination, when all 18 dead soldiers had been returned to home base, revealed that their genitals had also been removed. The surgical procedure must have been performed quite some time after the death of the victims because there was no evidence of bleeding. A crude bandage had been used on each dead body and then, its clothing put back on to provide an element of surprise for the medical personnel.

An investigation by military police was underway, but no progress had yet been reported.

In the city of Melbourne, Australia, yet another incident was reported at the swimming pool of a luxury hotel early in the morning on October 25th. Six more bodies of White males were discovered floating face down in the pool by the maintenance crew as they started the day's chores. All six had been injected with deadly cyanide poison and were dumped into the swimming pool during the night, so as to panic the visiting tourists when the bodies were found. Yes— the victims were also castrated in a manner which was becoming a trademark for the terrorist group responsible for these barbaric acts.

Whites living in outposts around the world where Whites were a small minority felt especially threatened. The vulnerability to attack by their host nations, placed them in a reverse bias situation. Already, tales of mass executions of White people by terrorist groups operating at night filtered back with increasing frequency.

In Hong Kong, alone, as many as 50 colonists of British ancestry were massacred in the White section of the city during one raid by a group of racial extremists. On this occasion, the victims included females as well as males, and some were children. Bodies were found brutally beaten, and in a few cases – beheaded. The males were castrated, indicating a connection with the other ongoing atrocities in the world.

Singapore had an even more gruesome experience during the night when over a 100 British subjects, male and female, were beaten to death and butchered to pieces. Heads, arms, legs, and torso, were scattered around a city square and nearby streets in plain view for horrified city dwellers to discover the next morning.

Hideous crimes took place at a steady rate, which showed no indication of ceasing. The White race was under siege by an enemy strongly assumed to be nonwhite; but nobody knew whether the acts of terrorism were committed by renegade groups operating in various areas of the globe, or through an organized effort. In any case, the viciousness and telltale symbol of infertility sent the message that the ultimate result hoped for was extinction.

The Black populace of Cape Town, South Africa, was the first race to show contempt publicly for Whites. It was touted as vindication for centuries of being ruled through oppression by foreigners and suffering untold inhumanities, not the least of which was being enslaved. Executions of Whites by hanging, usually during the night, took place over wide areas of the city. Like a zebra being stalked by a lion, so, too when a White person wandered away from protective cover, he or she was felled.

The news coming out of South Africa was of a violent Black revolt. Rumors were that a bloodbath was taking place as the White minority defended itself, with the death toll estimated to be heading towards the thousands.

There was no doubt now that around the globe a genocide was taking place. The White race had been selected for extinction and subjected to atrocities of all types. Even though the total number of Whites slaughtered, so far, didn't represent a significant percentage of the planet's White population; signs were seen for an escalating purge. A holocaust could easily develop making the entire White race the victim, if the rest of the world, with an overwhelming superiority in numbers should become united in such a monstrous cause.

It was still assumed that what was happening was the work of a few extremists, although they appeared to be well organized for their activities to have been so widespread. All acts of terrorism, with the exception of the Black revolt in South Africa, had been of a subversive nature, and there had not even been a clue that could possibly identify the guilty parties.

Several rays of hope shone for Western World nations fearing that the White race had been targeted for extermination. In the United Nations, every government denied connection with the sinister acts of terrorism and denounced their occurrence. Around the world, people of all races held rallies against the violence, appalled that such barbarism still existed in a civilized society. Across the globe, law enforcement organizations did their utmost to quell riots and discourage racist activities. They also intensified their own investigations to locate the perpetrators.

The morale of the citizens of the Western World reached a low ebb since the onset of the terrible atrocities. White people felt insecure and at a loss as to how to interpret such frightening global events. The euphoria of a few months ago, related to miraculous medical developments extending one's lifespan, unaccompanied by crippling illness, dispersed.

In a move to reduce the chance of further bloodshed, if at all possible, Western nations issued an advisory to their citizenry to curb foreign travel where they would be most vulnerable to attack. Also, voluntary evening curfews were strongly recommended, even in predominantly White areas normally considered safe. It was hoped that the chance of surprise assaults would be minimized by self-imposed restrictions.

The White race was in a struggle for its own survival where the outcome at this particular time appeared gloomy. Whites had become prey to unidentifiable predators who may have been members of a terrorist organization—or quite possibly his own nonwhite fellow humans. Taking a long view of the situation, one may wonder what a person of Native American heritage may have thought about current events...

16

Isolated in the ivory tower of university life, Louis Keck was preoccupied with his research program. Totally engrossed in his own work, he was oblivious to the terrorist activities victimizing members of his own race in all parts of the world. The prime coverage of each atrocity sort of played in the background of his mind. A dedicated scientist, his primary concern was to develop a practical mathematical model of a thermo-nuclear fusion reaction.

During the past several months, Lou modeled different approaches to plasma particle behavior, and none of these worked out to his satisfaction. His main objective was to have a mathematical expression with continuity so that extrapolation in time could be performed on it, to predict an expected reaction once initiated.

Lou came up with numerous models that more or less represented how a thermo-nuclear reaction progressed, but in every case, after bouncing the ideas off his colleagues at the institute, he ruled them out because of various flaws. Of all the configurations tried so far, he convinced himself that each one failed to adequately fit the process either because of a violation of a physical principle or the lack of agreement with experimental data.

This kind of work was new to Louis, and he wondered if he might be spending the taxpayers' money reinventing the wheel to no avail. He found it stimulating to work side by side with specialists in the field of thermo-nuclear physics, but was beginning to doubt where he might make a contribution. His own expertise, the area of feedback control, appeared remote from the science of particle physics.

During his years in industry, Lou had made use of the so-called classical approach when modeling physical processes. Somehow, the important parameters were accounted for, and there was a convenient principle of physics to predict behavior. The ultimate solution to problems made use of fundamental concepts known to be accurate, so it was easy to tailor the solution to fit the problem exactly. The terms in the mathematical model of a process that didn't appear significant could usually be ignored without serious penalty in performance. Such was the approach philosophy to solving problems. The degree of complexity was usually intentionally limited to provide what was considered an elegant solution to a problem.

The environment that Lou found himself in was one where probability played a major role. The fusion research currently concentrated on ways of increasing the odds of fusion actually taking place. The chance happening of two hydrogen nuclei fusing together to form a helium atom while also releasing a chunk of energy was dependent upon the preconditions created to make it possible.

The fusion process itself was a violent reaction because of the extremely large amount of energy released. It self-destructed in a fraction of a second because the preconditions necessary to bring about the process could not be maintained. The force of the explosion as the number of reacting nuclei avalanches upward was so great that containment became impossible, and the entire process stopped almost as fast as it started.

Such was the dilemma that Lou faced: a choice between a highly complex analysis, which required rigorous mathematical treatment, and a not so complex approach, more easily handled from a practical viewpoint, but one that might not yield answers –the reason for his efforts in the first place.

Okay, I figure that the mechanism which stops a fusion reaction from a complete "burning" of all hydrogen within the reactor propagates from the outside inward, so my analysis will be different from that of other explosives. Let's say, from gunpowder in a cartridge, and dynamite. They "burn" completely once ignited or triggered.

The blast of the explosion is very dependent on the mode of burning of the reacting material. The cartridge in a gun or the confined stick of dynamite, once triggered, can be thought of as a two-step process where complete "burning" takes place first. The blast outward follows as the second step.

In the case of the fusion reaction, containment fails before the reaction is complete. However, because fusion is taking place all the way out to the outer boundary of the reactor, the force outward being produced by the entire reactor is to a certain extent counteracted by an inward force generated by all fusing material which is away from dead center of the reactor. The effect of this inward force is to momentarily further compress the hydrogen toward the center of the reactor, so as to extend its "burning" time. Unlike the instant "burning" of the gunpowder and dynamite, there is a tailing off in the fusion process, which shapes the impulse outward comprising the blast, to give it more duration instead of an abrupt decrease to zero.

The comparison between conventional explosives and a thermo-nuclear reaction in the time domain shows two very different time scales. For conventional devices, the entire process could last probably as long as a thousandth of a second. On the other hand, a fusion reaction may last no longer than a trillionth of a trillionth of a second.

The time duration of the Big Bang is thought to have been of that order of magnitude. However, the distribution of mass in our expanding universe resulting from that Big Bang surely was affected greatly by the shape of the impulse that caused the explosion.

Lou was completely absorbed, mentally examining all he knew of the fusion process so far and deciding what the next step in his research program should be, when Charlie Stafford walked in.

"Good morning, Lou, how's everything today?"

"Not so well, Charlie. I seem to be running around in circles lately. I'm not sure you have the right man for this job. Why did you hire a guy like me in the first place, Charlie?"

"Come now, Lou—it can't be all that bad. I wanted you because I wanted the best man for this new activity— and I didn't say it was going to be easy.

"We've been researching controlled fusion to death for years. Why? Because it's the way of the future, and some day fusion energy will be our lifeline if man is to survive on this planet.

"I don't need to lecture you about something you already know, Lou. What I need to impress upon you is the importance of the work you have been doing."

"I hear what you're saying, Charlie, but you already have people on your staff that are at least ten times more qualified for this work than I could ever hope to be."

"That's where you are wrong, Lou— I don't have one man on my staff with the creative engineering background that you have. Furthermore, in the few short months that you've been with us, you have gained the respect of every person on my staff – no exceptions.

"You may not realize it, but many of my people are starting to think more and more like engineers because of your very presence at this lab – and I can assure you that they are enjoying it.

"You've brought a new purpose to the efforts of my research team. Each one of my guys is a qualified specialist in his own field of interest, but now, he sees the contributions made by his colleagues, and he has a better feel for what our ultimate goals are."

"You are being very kind to me, Charlie, but I have the feeling, sometimes, like I am bucking a stone wall.

"I'm trying to model a process that is very complex by using simple-minded concepts – and that's where the rub comes in. It may be that what I'm attempting to do is just not possible."

"Rest assured we appreciate your efforts, Lou, and we're all confident that you are the right man for this job. Just continue what you are doing – we're all in this together. Does that sound alright to you?"

"OK, if you say so, Charlie. I'll do my darnedest; thanks for dropping by."

After his meeting with Charlie, Lou felt somewhat relieved. Maybe he was serving a purpose at the Fusion Lab. Coming out of retirement as he had, his new career had to present him with a challenge, and there was no doubt that it did. Taming of the fusion process was like handling a tiger by the tail – you never knew when it would turn around and bite you. There was no question that progress would be difficult to come by, and many false starts experienced along the way.

Later in the day, Lou made his daily call to Katy, to find out how she was managing the home front. "What are we having for dinner tonight, Hon?" This was his standard opening question.

"You're such a predictable guy, always thinking about food. Do stuffed shells and a tossed salad sound alright to you, Dear? Don't forget, it's your tennis night; I know how important that is to you."

The two of them gabbed for five minutes or so about not much of anything, but they enjoyed talking to each other.

"I have to go now, Hon. Dinner sounds good to me. We haven't had shells for quite some time. I should be home around 5:30. Bye now."

"Stuffed shells, huh?" Lou muttered to himself after he hung up. *That woman has a knack for coming up with the right words at the most appropriate times.* A new idea crossed his mind, and he jotted it down.

Up to now, he had concentrated on variations of individual particle behavior and then on a homogeneous plasma inside the fusion envelop when defining a mathematical model.

The idea of concentric shells could provide the symmetry that he was looking for. Closely packed spherical shells of sizes ranging from the smallest at zero diameter to the largest at the diameter of the reacting volume, all contained inside each other, would comprise the fusion reactor itself.

If I can develop this concept, I'll have the necessary mobility in this model to follow step-by-step as the fusion reaction takes place. The shell approach could make it possible to introduce a plasma gradient starting outward from the center of the reactor, where at each shell, a different set of conditions will exist.

It should be possible to represent mathematically, the progression of the fusion explosion from the time it's triggered to the point in time when it no longer sustains itself. The fusion scenario would go something like…well, in the case of a hydrogen bomb, the compression and subsequent containment of the fusion reactor by an imploding fission reaction as a trigger, makes the onset of fusion possible. Then as the fusion energy is released uncontrollably in an avalanching fashion, and the internal pressure surges, a point is reached when containment is no longer possible. The expanding reactor loses its ability to maintain fusion because the conditions necessary to make it possible are disappearing. The release of fusion energy ceases as the process comes to an abrupt stop, just a split second after it starts.

The moment of interest is that split second when fusion takes place. Initially, the hydrogen atoms fuse together to form helium throughout the reaction volume. Then, as internal pressure builds up due to the rapid release of energy, the outer most shell of the reacting volume feels the entire thrust of the explosion, and its diameter begins to grow in size. It carries along the hydrogen atoms within its own walls. These atoms no longer are under enough pressure to sustain fusion. Successively, each new outer shell undergoes the same experience until the entire reacting volume has disappeared.

What that says is that fusion does not stop instantaneously throughout the reacting volume. Instead, the stoppage seems to propagate from the outside inward. The entire process is by no means 100% efficient because a substantial amount of the hydrogen never gets to fuse into helium.

At this point, Lou felt keyed up about having a new idea to work on. He finally had a good picture in his own mind that he could relate to. *Now, if I can explain it on paper in mathematical terms...*

First things first, let's get a generalized model put together that can accommodate a wide range of constants and parameter test values for simulation on the computer.

Lou returned home excited, feeling he just might be on the right track.

"How was your day at the office, Dear?" Katy asked as she greeted him at the door. "You sounded in a hurry to hang up during our conversation. Did someone pop in on you unannounced and you had to cut it short?"

"No, No, Hon, not at all – it was something you said about stuffed shells that launched my mind on to a whole new track.

"As you know, I've been searching for an approach to this fusion problem, and you hit the nail right on the head!"

"Really? What did I say that wound you up so? You look, as the saying goes, like the cat that swallowed the canary. What's the big secret going through your head? Please, let me in on it, Dear."

"It's no big deal, Hon; it's the way you said it that counts. When you mentioned shells, it struck a chord in my darn head that suddenly took me all the way back to my calculus days at college, back 40-some years ago. We were taught to use thin concentric shells in deriving formulas for volumes of all kinds of geometric shapes, such as spheres, and the like."

"What's that got to do with the Fusion Lab? I don't see the connection."

"It just so happens that I can use the same technique to describe the inner workings of an H Bomb – or even the Big Bang of creation. Don't you see the outstanding contribution you just made to science, Honey? Your name will become famous in the years to come – and I'll be referred to as your spouse."

Katy laughed. "I don't understand what you are talking about, but I'll accept the accolades, anyway. Aren't you glad you married me?"

"Yes – I am one lucky guy." Lou hugged and kissed his wife, and they enjoyed a good laugh. "Now, what's for supper again?" he asked, which prompted another round of laughing.

During the weeks that followed, Lou could have used a bed at the labs, because he was there seven days a week working all kinds of odd hours. He kept in constant touch with members of Charlie's staff, checking and rechecking concepts in physics to make sure he was not violating any of the physical principles. He had system analysts from the institute's computing operations developing software.

Charlie Stafford got curious about the level of activity related to Lou's project.

"When you get hot on something, you don't let up, do you? You've been burning the candle at both ends for a few weeks now, Lou. I can only guess that you're making giant strides forward on this new idea of yours. Can you give me a status report on your progress so we can include it in the next quarterly report on our contract? The schedule calls for it to be in the hands of the Department of Energy two weeks from today."

"No problem, Charlie. In fact, I'm glad you stopped by to remind me, because lately I've been losing track of time. When you pulled me out of retirement, I never told you that there would be times like this when I'd lose contact with the rest of the world," Lou said, with an obvious smile of accomplishment.

Charlie sensed that Lou had not been spinning his wheels and the recent activity had been producing results.

"How's your shell concept coming along? Judging by the feedback from the fusion staff, you may be on the verge of a breakthrough?"

"First, let me temper your observations and your expectations just a wee bit, Charlie, because I'm sure that what we've been doing is most likely not original in this particular field. I may have been selfish in trying to educate myself on the subject of nuclear physics; I greatly appreciate the patience your staff has shown while tutoring me on the subject. Let's keep in mind that this a simulation of a fusion reaction and it does not consider the necessary preamble to make it happen."

"Don't worry about that, Lou. All I've heard from these guys has been enthusiasm about your project. Please, go on – I want to hear what you have to say."

"OK, Charlie. You asked for it. We've been debugging our Big Bang program and hope to have it ready for simulation testing in another couple of weeks. Now – I call it the Big Bang program because it is a generalized program and I like to think that it could also be applicable to simulating the Big Bang of our universe's creation. I hope that's not interpreted as going off on a tangent in an area that's not even on our contract goals."

"No, not a problem, Lou, because although we didn't specifically mention Big Bang in the proposal, we committed ourselves to developing a simulation model of a fusion reaction.

"I interpret that to mean a general purpose model, which is all inclusive of fusion devices. No doubt, the Big Bang fits in that category."

"With that obstacle, cleared, let me introduce another one," said Lou. "I did not concern myself with how fusion is brought about. I assumed that it wouldn't make any difference whether an imploding fission trigger or a gravitational collapse, such as in the Big Bang – here we go again – was used.

"In my program, the clock starts ticking at the instant when plasma compression has been applied and fusion gets underway. Then all hell breaks loose.

"Again, I'm assuming that the main interest is during the fusion process itself."

"Exactly what I was hoping your reasoning would be, Lou. There's no point in over-complicating the model with more discontinuities. What you are doing zero's right in on the main event. I like it. Keep going."

"We're using a color graphics terminal to show fusion in progress from time zero. The screen display will show a two dimensional slice through the center of the reactor which will be at the center of the screen.

"The process under study has spherical symmetry; therefore, the picture viewed on the screen will not be distorted as long as the sample slice cuts dead center through the reactor.

"The color graphics are used to indicate the level of thermal activity in different parts of the reactor. Where there is fusion, the color will be white hot and decreasing into violet. Then, as conditions for fusion are no longer met, the color temperature will change from blue, to green, to yellow, and then to red, where rapid expansion is taking place with corresponding fast cooling.

"We are also using time expansion in the simulation to slow down the dynamics of the process to allow viewing at different time intervals during fusion. The simulated time multiplier will be selectable over a wide range up to a trillion, trillion, or ten raised to the twenty-fourth power. Maximum run duration in terms of viewing time will be in the neighborhood of a few seconds.

"There are two modes of operation which are selectable. The first is the dynamic mode for continuous viewing from start to finish. This mode is mainly to show how the reactor transitions from full power at the onset of fusion to zero power when conditions no longer exist to support fusion.

"The second mode is a sampling mode which provides for stop motion at any time or at preselected intervals to examine the pictorial display. In this mode, the cursor can be positioned at any place on the screen to obtain a measurement of plasma density as a direct readout on the screen."

"How flexible is this system going to be for setting up different sets of conditions?" asked Charlie. "Also, how complex will be the operation of the program? Will the operator have to be a specially trained individual?"

"We did our utmost to make the system operation as user friendly as possible, Charlie. The program is menu operated every step of the way from the initial setup of the test run to the data sampling during the run.

"Initial conditions such as the quantity of heavy hydrogen injected into the reactor chamber and the amount of compression applied to start the process are all called for in the menu.

"You can see where the operator is calling the shots every step of the way."

"I am truly impressed, Lou. This is a very ambitious project, and from the looks of what's been done so far, I would say you are doing a commendable job.

"Our quarterly report will be a very interesting one this time around. Don't be surprised if we get a batch of visitors from Washington before too long.

"Keep up the good work, and please keep me posted on developments." Charlie was obviously very pleased with Lou's progress and gave him a sincere handshake as he left to touch base with other staff members.

The next two weeks were a hectic period for Louis as he put the final touches on his simulation of a fusion reaction.

The system analysts assigned to him were dedicated professionals who had done an excellent job of developing his software. Lou considered the successful outcome of his project to have been a team effort and made sure that everyone who participated got to share in the credit – including his wife Katy.

The day of the big in-house demonstration arrived and the staff members gathered in the machine room around the Cray super computer console. If all went well, this would be the first of many such demonstrations for interested parties in the field of nuclear physics and engineering.

Lou had called the meeting, so he presided over the test runs prepared for the demonstration.

"Ladies and gentlemen – and of course my dear wife, Katy – welcome to fantasy land. This is the first group showing of our fusion simulator to which many of you have contributed during its development. Herb Wilson, who led the software development effort, will serve as console operator for this simulation. I see where Herb is already on station – ready for the fireworks.

"We will limit today's demonstration to the dynamic mode of operation because the sampling mode which involves stop action for data sampling and such would be too time consuming. Now, to give you an idea of how our series of tests will proceed, we will run a sequence of runs in the dynamic mode, where each run will be nonstop from start to finish. Each of these runs might last for as long as two or three seconds in expanded time – or real time as far as you are concerned.

"Since there are many combinations of initial conditions possible, we certainly can't try them all today. Instead, we've chosen to fix the containment compression at a level we know is adequate for a reaction. Then the sequence of runs will start off with a sub-critical amount of hydrogen, which is not enough to undergo any fusion. Each following run in the sequence will have a 50% increase in hydrogen.

"The six by six projection that you see on the wall in front of us is a magnified replica of Herb's CRT display. White and violet will indicate fusion and the first time you see it will be at the center of the screen. All other colors from blue to red indicate temperatures not high enough for fusion."

"Herb – please take over from here starting with the sub-critical run. And can someone please turn off the lights before we start?"

As expected, the first couple of runs produced only red on the screen.

Then as the hydrogen amount was increased, a color shift took place, and the rainbow colors from red at the outer boundary to blue at the center started appearing.

Then, it happened. First violet and then intense white light appeared as a small dot at the center of the screen and quickly disappeared into the center.

"Yeah! Wow! Look at that!" Loud cheers from the crowd and Katy beaming at him, signaled approval.

Each succeeding run produced a spontaneous ever-larger circular white area centered on the screen. The tail end of each run gripped everyone's attention. The white area was seen to shrink in diameter as it was replaced by the rainbow colors; and it finally disappeared into the center of the screen. The phenomenon seemed to confirm Lou's earlier theory that the stoppage of fusion propagates inward from the outer boundary of the reactor. Further increases in hydrogen don't seem to affect the kaleidoscope of color except for brighter and sharper color tones.

The first demonstration was meant to startle the audience in a stroke of showmanship, which it certainly accomplished. However, the use of the simulator as a research tool was just beginning.

After the completion of the monumental, contracted task, Lou and Katy took a well-earned vacation to the Gulf coast at Brownsville, right there in Texas. Katy had managed to swap a week of their timeshare condominium in Aruba for one in Brownsville. Mid-October was considered an ideal time of the year for the beach in that part of the country.

Actually, Katy had another reason for picking a spot closer to home in the continental US. The almost daily reports of terrorist attacks against White people all over the world was enough to scare anyone.

Why such horrible crimes, she kept wondering, and hoped she could turn off her fear long enough to enjoy her husband's "return."

17

During the month of October, the entire world was preoccupied by ongoing acts of terrorism committed against the White race. Whoever was behind the atrocities, whether an organized group of terrorists or renegade members of nonwhite races out to punish Whites, the effect was devastating. Everyone wondered if the White race might possibly be doomed and its days on the planet numbered.

While the turmoil went on in every part of the globe, no one noticed another major change that had stealthily taken place: Hospital baby nurseries had become populated entirely by nonwhites.

Hospital staffs across North America never thought that something out of the ordinary might be happening. After all, past experience had shown wide fluctuations in the races of newborn infants on a day-to-day basis. The racial mix of babies occupying nurseries had been known to swing in all directions: all White to all Black or all Asian at certain times, to a uniform or random mix at others. The present situation was just one of those cyclical variations that frequently happened.

Not until European countries reported zero White birth rates since the middle of October did Americans finally become aware of a global problem. Particular Scandinavian countries essentially reported zero births because of their homogeneous populations.

Record checking at most of the large American hospitals showed an abrupt drop to zero of White births within a four-day period starting in late October. By the end of the month, the situation had shown no sign of returning to normal, except for a handful of White births.

The United States government purposely downplayed this totally unexpected turn of events and assured the citizenry that there was nothing to worry about, in an attempt to prevent people from panicking. The medical authorities from the Surgeon General's Office were aware of a serious problem that could have long-term implications. Was the White race destined to become extinct?

Scientists in the medical field were already deeply in thought considering potential causes for the sudden sterility in White people.

Members of the clergy could not help but wonder if the wrath of God might have been aroused by White man's extravagant lifestyle and sometimes, blatant defiance of religious dogma. Quite possibly, the multitude of methods developed for birth control might be viewed by the Creator as tampering with Nature's ways.

Might there be a connection between events that had happened since the beginning of the year? Many Whites went from a state of exhilaration from the discovery of its resistance to serious diseases to one of gloom over its loss of ability to procreate.

Tom Curtis, over in Brunswick, Maine, had been pondering these events with a good amount of interest, naturally because of his own Molly's involvement.

"How long ago was it that you and I rode down to Boston for the meeting at Gerber? I mean the one where you took part in their chemotherapy test program?" Tom asked Molly, as she set up slides of tissue samples for him to view under the microscope. Since her recovery, Molly had taken a part-time job at the college as an assistant in the pathology lab.

"Funny you should ask that question, Honey. I'll never forget. It was on January 14th, this year, and I was such a wreck at the time – remember?"

"Yes, I know, but that was also about the time when you started to feel better – we can't forget that.

"Listen to this. I just had a notion that maybe there's a connection between your miraculous recovery and the zero birth rates being experienced now.

"Mid-October, which is the period when the number of White babies being born suddenly dropped to zero, is also nine months since mid-January."

"I can see the wheels turning in that smart head of yours, already. Are you telling me the same thing that started me on the road to recovery nine months ago is also what is preventing White women from getting pregnant?"

"That's exactly what I'm saying, Moll. The two are related through genetics.

"Somehow, the White race suddenly acquired a unique property which is beneficial on the one hand and disastrous on the other. We have our work cut out for us to perform some very fundamental research in a race against time."

"Oh my God, Tom. Could we only have about one generation of time to come up with answers? You don't think the White race could actually vanish from the face of the Earth, do you?"

"As of this moment, we have become an endangered species," Tom said, looking as alarmed as his wife.

Tom was being realistic in his appraisal of a monumental problem. He could envision a massive effort in the field of genetics, to find the answers.

Tom Curtis was not the only man of science who had been awakened to the dire problem. Bob Armstrong was also seriously thinking about what could be affecting mankind in such drastic ways.

He was well aware of the sudden onset of overwhelmingly successful transplants in January. Since then he had performed numerous organ transplants on White patients without any complications whatsoever as compared to similar surgeries on nonwhites with the usual postoperative problems necessitating the use of anti-rejection drugs.

It didn't take him long to make the correlation between when these successes began and when White women started experiencing infertility. In his reasoning, however, there was a small glitch he couldn't explain. Ben Davidson, one of his heart transplant patients, had a White wife who was as pregnant as could be.

As a follow up to his line of thinking, Bob called up Ben at the NASA Space Center to inquire about Mary's status.

"Hi Ben, this is Bob Armstrong calling. I hope I'm not interrupting you in your work."

"Not at all, Doctor. What can I do for you?"

"I trust you are still in good spirits and that your health is holding up well, Ben. I'm certainly interested in your wellbeing, but this time, I would like to inquire about your wife, Mary. She is expecting soon – am I right?"

"I get the picture, now, Doc. The baby is due on February 6th, coming up, and you are wondering how it was at all possible for her to get in the family way.

"To tell you the truth, the same thought crossed my mind. There are usually exceptions to most strange phenomena; I guess Mary and I happen to be the ones. What else can I say?"

"Have you read about the latest findings where biracial people are unaffected by this infertility? Latinos in the Western Hemisphere, known to be a blend of Spanish, Indian, and sometimes Black, are showing no signs of interruption in their birth rates. The same appears true with some Arab tribes in the Middle East and North Africa. These people are believed to be mixtures of White, African, and possibly even Asian races.

"What I'm wondering, Ben, is this. Do either you or Mary have trace amounts of races other than White in your family backgrounds?"

"Now, that could be a loaded question, Doc, but let me answer you this way, and don't feel that I take offense because racial prejudice isn't my style. I understand you are covering all the bases and what you are asking is very possible.

"However, I have to disappoint you on this one. Mary is from a long line of Norwegians that settled in Minnesota back in the 1800's. Unless her Viking ancestors brought back nonwhite brides when returning from their long voyages; I'd say she's a good bet for being a purebred.

"As for myself, my background is English and my ancestors were settlers in the Connecticut sailing port of New London. My genealogy is English on both sides dating back to days of the Puritans."

"Well, that shoots down my theory. I guess you and Mary really are the exception to the rule. Thanks for the information anyway, Ben, and give my regards to Mary.

"I'll be seeing you on January 14th for the anniversary checkup on your new heart – right? Goodbye now." And Robert Armstrong hung up, still curious how it was possible for Mary Davidson to be pregnant.

Louis and Katy Keck, had just returned from their Brownsville trip when they got the word about the zero White birthrate.

"There sure is a lot happening in the world these days," Katy remarked as she scanned the front page of the newspaper. "Do you think that the end of the world is near? It almost looks like the White race is in limbo."

"I have to agree with you, Hon. There are some very strange goings-on, which could really get a person to do some basic thinking. I wonder if all these events are related. Maybe our day of reckoning has arrived and these are the first signs of what is ahead."

"Don't talk like that, Lou. It's scary when I think of what could happen to the children – and not least of all, our grandchildren. It gets pretty gloomy when you think about what the future holds for them – if there is to be a future." Tears came into Katy's eyes.

"Come now, Honey, I was only using a figure of speech. Don't be so sad; there has to be a satisfactory explanation for what's been happening. We must hold on to our faith in human nature.

"And there's bound to be a stepped up effort in all branches of science to come up with answers – and they will – don't you worry."

"Of course, of course you're right," Katy said, drying her eyes with a tissue.

"I see this as an opportunity to extend my present work at the lab to a subject that has been one of my lifelong ambitions. I'm talking about a study of the Big Bang. Remember how you steered me in the right direction, just a short time ago?"

Katy felt comforted because she believed her husband in bad times as well as in good. During their years together, Lou had been a good family man as well as a dedicated man of science. Now in their advanced years, Katy felt a continuing love and admiration for him that always made the future look promising, regardless of how much uncertainty loomed. Whatever future surprises Nature may have for mankind, she and her husband would face them together.

In spite of the efforts and good intentions of the scientific community, the mood of White citizenry of the world over rapidly deteriorated to one of utter hopelessness. Apparently, the acts of terrorism committed against Whites were a preamble to the main event. Genocide by sterilization was the ultimate method of assuring permanent elimination of a species. And headlines did nothing to assuage anyone's fears.

```
THE BIRTH RATE OF WHITES
REMAINS AT ZERO!!!!
THE WHITE RACE IS DOOMED!!!!
```

18

NOVEMBER

The desperate plight of the White race did not engender compassion from the terrorists responsible for the ongoing atrocities. Instead, they appeared to interpret the sudden zero birth rate as an omen signaling that they were not moving rapidly enough in their efforts to exterminate the undesirable White race. Accordingly, they chose to intensify their acts of violence by going for much bigger stakes. On November 14th, events set off a new phase.

An Aeroflot passenger jet on its way to Moscow from Berlin exploded at thirty-five thousand feet over Krakow, Poland. There were no survivors among the 218 passengers and 6 crew members. A check of the flight dossier from the last stop in Vienna, Austria, listed only White people on board the aircraft.

Pieces of the plane were scattered about the countryside in a farming region. Fragments of the poor victims were strewn across fields, covering an area of over a square mile. There was no doubt the explosion that caused the disaster was immense. The only recognizable pieces of the airplane to be found were the tail section and parts of the wings, along with pieces of the landing gear. The fuselage, including the cockpit section, was totally obliterated.

When the flight recorder was finally located in a pasture, the contents of the flight log confirmed the cause of the accident. Every critical parameter being recorded indicated normal behavior up to an exact instant when all channels went blank.

A bomb had been placed on board the aircraft, either at the point of origin, which was Berlin, or Vienna – the only stop on the way to Moscow. Further checking revealed there were two ticket-holding individuals in Berlin that checked in three pieces of luggage thru to Moscow, but failed to board the aircraft. The names of the two persons who never occupied their reserved seats were an Akim Assad and Rick Wang, listed as clothing manufacturers on a business trip. These names were most likely fictitious and probably intended to convey nonwhite nationalities.

The lack of clues at the crash site did not help to determine the specifics of the tragic accident. Based on circumstantial evidence, the conclusion was reached: another act of terrorism, indicating an escalation in the war against the White race.

One week later, on November 21st, a 747 jumbo jet of Transatlantic Airways on its way from New York to Paris exploded over the Mid-Atlantic. The horrible explosion was seen from shipboard by crewmen on a freighter almost directly below. This time there were 287 passengers and crewmen aboard; again, no survivors. The pieces of the airplane, once they hit the water, quickly sank to the depths of the ocean floor. Testimony of the seamen that saw the explosion left little doubt that it was another act of terrorism. The fact that the flight recorder was irretrievable was mute.

The airplane had been a charter flight originating in New York from Kennedy International Airport carrying a tour group of Americans of Scandinavian descent on their way to board the Euro-train for a one-month tour of Scandinavian countries. Not surprisingly, all passengers were White, even the eight crew members.

There was no sure explanation of how a bomb could have been placed on board. It's possible that it was snuck into a passenger's luggage at an opportune time without his cognizance just prior to check-in time; or it could have been carried aboard the aircraft by someone disguised as a member of the maintenance crew during preflight operations. Either way, there was no evidence to pinpoint the cause of the terrible accident.

The White race was engaged in a struggle for survival against an unknown enemy striking fatal blows anywhere in the world at a time of his choosing. More and more White people felt like the targets of a sniper. There were no warnings of impending attacks or acts of sabotage, but the message was unmistakably clear: a well-organized group of terrorists or far out racial fanatics was committing genocide.

Three days later, on November 24th, a luxury vacation ship of the Norwegian Cruise Line departed Miami for a two-week Thanksgiving Caribbean cruise. The itinerary included stops in San Juan, St. Thomas, St. Martins, Barbados, Aruba, and a last stop at the Cayman Islands before completing the circle around Cuba back to Miami.

After the stopover at Aruba, all contact with the ship was lost. Three days later, it was spotted by a search plane about a 150 miles south of the Caymans, apparently adrift. Attempts to establish radio contact with the ship were unsuccessful.

A few hours later, a rescue ship arrived at the scene with a boarding party to investigate. The rescuers found no one on deck. However, once they went below deck to the living quarters, they were in for a shocking discovery. Dead bodies of the crew and passengers were everywhere. There were no signs of a struggle; the corpses had the appearance of having just gone to sleep.

It didn't take long to realize that poison gas had been used in a mass execution, probably during the night after people had retired, because many wore their nightclothes. Of the twelve hundred and fifty-one dead people counted, all were White, except for eleven Black crew members and seven others of Asian background. There were no survivors. Since the ratio of White victims to others was so disproportionate, it was assumed to also be an act of terrorism.

Investigation by chemical warfare personnel confirmed the suspicion of poison gas having been the mass murder weapon. Autopsies performed on some of the bodies indicated the use of a nerve gas, which had caused instant paralysis when first inhaled and death moments later. The particular gas was known to be stockpiled by the superpowers of the world as a deterrent to war, but several countries were suspected of having it in their weapons arsenals. Like most weapons used in warfare, chemical weapons were accessible on the black market or from arms peddlers who do a lucrative business with terrorist groups.

The efficiency of the method of killing people was chilling. If they were able to use nerve gas so successfully the first time, wasn't there a high probability it would be employed again and again in the future – but where?

On the ninth of December, the invisible terrorists struck again – this time, on an extensively used Trans-Siberian Railway passenger train. There were 911 passengers on board in fourteen cars, towed by two diesels. The train had been traveling east out of Moscow since early morning. The last stop where passengers were known to have detrained and others embarked was at the factory town of Chernov, about a hundred and fifty miles east of Moscow. An early winter was already being felt, and the temperature had dropped to near zero degrees Centigrade as the train left the station.

The train pulled into the station in Novograd, a busy terminal. Station porters and passengers stood in wait for the car doors to open. Nothing. Railroad personnel on the platform looked at each other quizzically. What was going on? No engineer stuck his head out, no other railroad attendants on board appeared. An eerie silence ensued.

Porters hopped on to the steps of the train between cars, released the locks, and climbed on board. Most of the passengers were slumped in their seats as if sleeping. It didn't take long to realize they were dead.

When authorities arrived to investigate, they discovered poison gas canisters in each of the railroad cars, hidden under a seat, with a timing device to release the gas at a preset time. There was no question that high-tech equipment and methods were employed to execute such an insidious act of terror. No clues were found to expose the guilty ones except for the striking similarity to the cruise ship incident in the Caribbean a few days earlier.

Only twenty-six of the victims were not White. Of Asian extraction, they were no doubt considered minor collateral damage in an otherwise successful attack. Now, there is no doubt that the terrorists were part of a global operation out to inflict as many White casualties as possible. It didn't escape most people around the globe that the poison gas method of mass execution was reminiscent of the Nazi holocaust. Fear of continued surprise attacks grew.

114

Meanwhile, the United Nations held sessions around the clock, to find a way to stop the heinous acts of terror. All member nations convincingly put forth their case of denials for participating in such monstrous and barbaric acts against humanity, although many countries from Asia and Africa did not argue against the obvious racial connection linking the terrible events of the past few months.

Globally, law enforcement organizations cooperated with each other in their search for evidence that might identify the terrorists. So far, no tangible clues had been uncovered; and in the meantime, the Western World grew anxious, awaiting the next attack.

In Canada, the small town of Munroe, Alberta, about a hundred miles east of Edmonton (population about 5,000) was targeted next by the insane felons. As a town, Munroe had been nonexistent prior to when oil was discovered at several cattle ranches and wildcatters appeared out of nowhere to do test drillings. The oil, like liquid gold, made many local ranchers instant millionaires.

Munroe was comprised of a refinery for processing the crude oil and a railroad terminal for shipping its products to locations all over North America. The residential section of the town was concentrated in a small area which had all the modern conveniences of a thriving community including a shopping mall. The people were mostly White middle and upper-middle class, earning a living off the oil industry.

During the night of December 12th, a trailer truck passed through town and workmen on the truck inconspicuously unloaded 55-gallon oil drums at 30 preselected locations covering the entire town. Then the truck headed out of town, south on Highway 44, but not without first being noticed by a police cruiser. Since the van had no special markings or logo on it, the policeman didn't pay special attention to it; it wasn't violating any laws.

No more than ten minutes after the truck left town, a timing device on each of the drums activated a valve, which quietly released lethal gas. In a matter of a minute or so, a blanket of colorless and odorless nerve gas covered the entire town.

While the poison gas traveled along air currents into the spaces between doors and windows of each home, the police desk sergeant's phone rang off the hook. Four calls from different areas in the town were identically alarming.

"You've got to come quick! I saw three people on the street, walking, and they just keeled over – I think they might be dead," a woman reported.

"I saw people on the street collapsing to the ground, they look unconscious!" said a man.

"Help, something's wrong here on 62 Maple Avenue. All of a sudden, three people outside just dropped to the ground – They look like they're turning blue!"

"Officer? Something strange is hap..." The fourth caller never finished their report.

The desk sergeant quickly issued an APB to the three cruisers on duty to investigate the four locations where the calls had come from – but abruptly went silent in the middle of providing details. The cruisers stayed in contact with each other by radio for as long as they were able to, until each one went quiet.

The remaining policeman had been the one who had spotted the trailer truck getting on the highway heading south. It just so happened that he was on the outskirts of town and away from the deadly blanket of nerve gas. His communication lines with the station and the other two cruisers had gone dead, and he was at a loss as to what to do. Luckily for him, he had pulled over his cruiser to think it through.

For some crazy reason, the trailer truck stuck in his mind. Apparently, the whole town had become a contaminated area, deadly to enter. What if there was a connection between the strange happenings and that darn truck?

Thoughts of what he should do raced through his head. He decided to follow a hunch. It had been 20 minutes since he spotted the truck; he should be able to catch up to it if he started the chase now. He couldn't risk driving through town, so he followed a perimeter road to avoid whatever danger lurked out there. He got on at the next entrance to the highway going south.

On the way to the highway, he radioed the Royal Mounted Police for assistance. They immediately set up a road barrier about 40 miles south of Munroe and hoped that the truck would go that far. They also dispatched a helicopter to patrol the highway in search of the trailer truck.

While the Munroe trooper raced south on Highway 44, the Royal Mounted Police waited at their barricade, flagging down approaching vehicles for inspection. They also had a backup in case the first barrier failed: an army tank, three miles down the road, poised in a straddling position across the two traffic lanes with its 75-millimeter gun pointed towards oncoming traffic. Vehicles which had been cleared were waved on through, by passing on the service lane.

After several minutes had gone by, the suspect trailer truck was sighted approaching the first stop at full speed.

The driver of the truck ignored the signal to stop and rammed his way through the barrier. His forward speed was hardly changed by the impact and he continued his southerly course.

About three minutes later, with several police cars chasing him, the driver of the truck spotted the tank directly in his path about two hundred yards in front of him. He was looking down the barrel of a cannon, and there was no question in his mind that he had to slam on the brakes. He came to a screeching halt no more than 20 feet from the tank.

A police bullhorn blared, "Everyone in the truck – come out with your hands above your heads."

Almost immediately, three gunshots were heard from inside the van.

Surprisingly, the driver and another rider in the cab slowly climbed down from the truck and were taken into custody. Three dead bodies are found inside the van, apparent suicides by a single, self-inflicted gunshot to the head.

Shortly after, the Munroe trooper arrived at the scene and felt relieved that he had listened to his instincts; although he still didn't know the extent of the tragedy in Munroe. When he finished relating his story to the Mounted Police, they headed towards the center of town in a convoy, expecting the worst.

As they approached Munroe, one of the prisoners was blabbing in broken English about danger ahead from poison gas. Help was requested from Edmonton Police who immediately sent chemical warfare special-ists by helicopter to rendezvous at the highway exit on the outskirts of town.

A three-man search party dressed in protective suits and carrying their own oxygen supply, drove into town and discovered a ghastly massacre. There were no survivors to be found, and a later body count of victims placed the death toll at 4,782.

Samples of residual gas were later identified as a nerve gas, which decomposed completely and became harmless about two hours after being released into the atmosphere. As a precautionary measure, the town was kept off limits until all the spent canisters were retrieved and the victims' bodies had been properly taken care of.

Interrogation of the two prisoners revealed that they were pro-fessional terrorists hired as mercenaries by a group of racial fanatics operating worldwide, whose self-appointed mission was to wipe the White race off the face of the Earth.

Out of the five accomplices, the survivors were from Egypt and China. The dead ones included a Black man, a Latino man, and a ren-egade member of the White race.

Further interrogation produced no additional information except for a display of extreme scorn for the White race, punctuated by blas-phemous outbursts of hatred. Their will to live must have given way to defiance as the two also took their own lives, without exposing the racial fanatics they worked for.

Undoubtedly, extreme hatred had simmered in the minds of the responsible fanatics for quite some time, pushed into boiling over at a final act of injustice. The events of the past year had provided exactly the right setting for putting in motion their grotesque scheme to rid the Earth of the detestable White race. It must have been unbearable to see the entitled Whites develop resistance to fatal illnesses and hear scientific reports supporting claims of White supremacy (espoused by the ignorant Fieldstone company), followed by the murderous act of the revived KKK.

Unless the racial fanatics responsible for the escalating acts of ter-rorism could be made to realize they were jeopardizing the survival of human life as a whole, the end of humanity on the planet loomed. The two biological changes which effected Whites remained pieces in a puzzle that urgently needed to be solved.

19

Ben Davidson's research in demography was coincidentally timely, given the momentous events taking place in the world. Surely, the effects of zero birth rate and the mounting number of casualties among White people due to the ongoing terrorists' activities would show up in the infrared monitoring of the Earth's surface by satellite.

NASA's polar orbiting satellite had been observing and charting the planet's rotating surface with orbiting infrared cameras once a day, for a good many years. The database represented accumulated surveys dating back to the late 1950's.

A usable infrared map of the world was realized about once per week, after signal averaging had been performed on the data to remove cyclical variation due to lack of synchronicity between the orbiting camera's speed and the rotating Earth. Even though a wide-angle lens was used, the camera never photographed exactly the same field on repeat passes.

The data stored was broadband within the infrared spectrum and originated from numerous sources on Earth. In fact, every object or body that had a temperature level radiated electromagnetic energy at a characteristic wavelength as a function of that temperature.

The next step was to separate out the human emission component. This was accomplished with a very sophisticated computer program that selectively picked out only that narrow infrared band representing the human element and rejected the rest. The end result would be a population map of the world with bright areas representing concentrations of people, such as in urban centers. Superimposing this map on top of a geographical map could confirm the expected population distribution on the globe.

Ever since Ben's return to work after his miraculous heart transplant operation, he was a human dynamo with one purpose in mind. He was obsessed with the idea of population monitoring using the novel concept.

"How soon do you expect to have a working program, Ben?" This was the question posed to him more frequently by management of late. Ben's superior, Fred Sherman, Section Manager of Computing Operations at NASA Houston, dropped by his office for a briefing on the project.

"You and your team have been attracting more and more attention since your return to work, and now the spotlight seems to be aimed directly at you," Tom said. "Isn't it ironic how word gets around with lightning speed when someone may be onto a new development?"

"I have good news for you this time around, Tom. With a few more refinements in our filtering subroutines, we should be able to run the full scale program by the end of this year. If we don't encounter too many glitches in our debugging efforts, we could be running with old data that will cover the time period up to January 1st.

"Tying into the real time global network will take another couple of months. Our data acquisition scheme has to be modified to accommodate the batch transmissions of raw data from relay stations around the globe."

"That's very encouraging, Ben, but don't you have another checkup with your doctor coming up by the end of the year? Do you think that could cause a postponement in the full scale testing?"

"Not at all, Tom, my scheduled appointment with Dr. Armstrong is on January 14th. If we don't run into a lot of trouble debugging the program, I am optimistic on at least some preliminary runs right after the New Year break."

"That's good to hear, with the world situation such as it is; there is a considerable amount of anxiety in various government circles right now. We'll be able to put the vast amount of infrared data we've accumulated to good use."

"I'll let you in on a little secret, Tom. The events of the past few months are really what has motivated me and my team to develop this infrared technique. There is nothing new to the idea; if it could be applied to crops for the purpose of estimating world food supplies, then there's no reason why the same technique shouldn't be useful to determine world population."

"Wild that every vegetable grown has its own infrared signature, and it becomes a simple matter to find out who is growing what and how much. So anything new to report on the TREND Program?"

"The only piece left to debug compares signal strengths at each location on the composite map representing population distribution for each frame and the succeeding frame. The frame-to-frame time is eight days, the amount of time needed to do the signal averaging. The difference in signal strengths at each location represents the change in population at that location during an eight day interval."

"Isn't an eight day period a very short time to be looking for a change in population? Your system resolution is probably too small to resolve very small differences."

"Good point, Tom. We've made provisions in the program to select time intervals in multiples of eight days, which should help amplify the small changes."

"I'll buy that. Now, how do you plan to present your results, Ben?"

"Let me backtrack a bit so I don't get ahead of myself. First off, we produce a population map that can be global, like a Mercator projection, which I'm sure you are familiar with from school geography where the entire planet is shown in one plane with maximum distortion at the North and South poles. For our purpose, the distortion does not bother us.

"The intent here is to overlay the population data on top of the geographical map as a concentration of bright dots, so that relative populations will show up as expected in urban and rural areas.

"The area coverage is not fixed to a global display. We also have the option of hemispherical, continental, or even mapping by country such as, Western Europe, the Far East, or the US by itself. Viewing can be on a projection screen from a color graphics terminal or a permanent hard copy can be generated by high speed plotter.

"All of this software has been completed and is operational. What remains to be done is to sum up the population data within the area under study and to compare that sample in time to a different sample at a later time.

"Relative increases or decreases in population will then be determined directly from the integrated infrared emissions seen by the orbiting satellite."

"That is one ambitious undertaking, Ben. Your progress has been phenomenal, but how do you plan to obtain an actual head count to establish population – from infrared data with any degree of confidence?"

"That's one we pondered for quite some time. It gets us into the question of system calibration, which gets complicated because of advancements in satellite technology, and units were launched into orbit over a period of years. Each camera system has its own sensitivity. But actually, there's a way to handle this problem. A bulk of the early data accumulated was obtained as a function of time. It's all dated, so it can be related to areas on Earth where populations during the corresponding time were precisely known.

"For example, certain large cities have kept up-to-date records of population for their own uses. We'll tap into that information to set up the scale factor automatically, for each camera to convert its own signal levels to numbers representing population.

"The next phase of our project, which will take about three more months, will deal with exactly that problem. We're calling it the CENSUS Program, and it will be a self-calibrating package, providing a continuous measure of population."

"Terrific. The TREND Program will be completed by the end of the year, and CENSUS should be ready about three months later."

"You got it, Tom. I hope to be able to show population trends and determine the impact of present world events."

"Thanks for the briefing, Ben. Your return to work has really motivated people around this place. Keep up the good work, and give us the word when you have something to show us." Fred Sherman left Ben's office on a note of optimism.

Ben realized he had set an ambitious goal for himself, especially at this particular time with Mary so close to her own expected delivery date.

On his way home from work, he couldn't help but wonder how his Mary even became pregnant. Last week's telephone call from Doc Armstrong concerning Mary had underscored his own curiosity. The birth rate of White people had been sitting at zero since mid-October; and here it was almost the end of the year with nothing happening to show a return to normalcy. And what about his own recovery from heart transplant surgery? That one didn't make sense either. Why would the White race all of a sudden be so tolerant of foreign organs used in transplant operations? What about the near disappearance of deadly diseases among Whites?

Ben had mixed emotions about all these events, and wasn't able to come up with a rational explanation except that fundamental changes were taking place in the world.

I wonder why Mary and I were granted a last chance at raising our own family after my being sick for so many years?

Mary greeted Ben at the door with her usual hug and kiss as he came in from the garage.

"How was your day, Dear? Did you have that meeting with Tom? He certainly must have been pleased with what you had to report."

"Yes, Hon. As a matter of fact, he was surprised our project had come along so far. Now, all of a sudden, we're on center stage with everyone anxiously looking at us, expecting all the answers. Really, I'm more concerned with your own condition right now. What did the doctor have to say when you visited him today?"

"Everything is fine and he thinks she will probably run full term which means about February 6th," Mary answered with a gleam in her eyes.

"What do you mean – 'she'? Have you been keeping secrets from me?" Ben was suddenly excited.

"I had an ultrasound done while I was at the hospital because Dr. Price thought it advisable to verify the baby's stage of development. That's how I found out. Aren't you happy, Dear?"

"It's great – you always said if you had a choice, you'd like a little girl the first time. Ben paused. "Is she normal?"

"Yes, yes, yes. Dr. Price said she looked as healthy as could be and for us not to worry. Aren't we lucky?"

"What are we going to name our new baby girl, Hon? Are we going to stick to our original choices? She'll have to live with it the rest of her life."

"I think Kristin Lea Davidson has a nice ring to it, don't you?"

"That settles it. Krissy it's going to be. I like it. I wonder if she'll be as dynamite as her mother."

Ben and Mary, obviously thrilled with the good news, hugged each other one more time. Only eight weeks of nervous anticipation left until little Krissy's arrival. But what kind of world was she being born into?

20

During the evening of December 18th, Christmas holiday traffic at Heathrow Airport in London was at its peak: travelers were either arriving or departing on trips to be with loved ones or going to faraway places to spend well-earned vacations.

Two businessmen inconspicuously maneuvered a large suitcase into the passenger waiting area for United Airlines. Unbeknownst to the hundreds of people coming and going around them, the men were terrorists and the "luggage" housed a nuclear device. If anyone had happened to look closely at them, they would have noticed the sweat beading on their foreheads.

As luck would have it, the bomb was a makeshift device that had never been tested. It was designed and built out of black market components, with few safety interlocks built in to guarantee proper sequencing of setup switches. This was its first application in their subversive acts of mass executions, and the men were novices in atomic weaponry, prone to make errors in setting the detonation time and properly arming the bomb.

Earlier in their van, the two had flipped switches at a feverish pace. The detonator for the shaped charges was set to go off at 10:45 PM. They would drive the plutonium wedges inward where critical mass would be reached and held momentarily to allow fission to take place. If all went according to plan, the magnitude of the blast would be about 40,000 tons of TNT. An explosion of that size was at least the equivalent of the Hiroshima bomb that drove Japan to surrender in 1945.

The terrorists made two mistakes.

In their rush to set up the atomic weapon, the men inadvertently overlooked the switch operation that made power available to the solenoid. There was no interlock to prevent that error, so when they flipped the switch to energize the solenoid – nothing happened – and there was no indication of their error. The atomic bomb never went off because of the lead blockage at the center of the core.

The second mistake was a bad oversight in not setting the time of day on the internal timer. The 10:45 time to detonate was correctly set, but by coincidence, the time of day on the timer was 10:44, giving them only one minute to make their way to the escape car.

They never made it. The explosive charge went off like imploding dynamite, which had a muffled sound; by the time it actually did blow apart, the force of the explosion was not nearly as great as it could have been.

Of all the people in the waiting room, the two terrorists were the closest and the relatively small blast knocked them unconscious with minor injuries. There were 24 other persons injured, but only 7 seriously. Luckily, no one was killed.

Those with a strong religious inclination knew it had to be an act of God that prevented a catastrophe from taking place. The terrorists must have overstepped their bounds and, a higher authority made His intervention to avert a man made disaster, which He no longer allowed, sympathetic to man's one-sided struggle for survival.

Had the nuclear explosion taken place, the casualties would surely have been counted in the many tens of thousands dead and about ten times that number seriously wounded. Many would have been slated to die from radiation-related illnesses.

The two accomplices captured turned out to be another Arab and a Korean. Upon their interrogation, they behaved much like the terrorists arrested after the Munroe slaughter. They refused to give information that could lead to the identity of their employers. Finally, they too, took their own lives, with hidden cyanide pills, and their secrets were buried with them.

Another tampering with atomic energy was about to take place near Erie, Pennsylvania, where a nuclear power facility supplied electricity to the North Atlantic states power grid. The date was December 23th, when everyone was in the holiday spirit with last minute preparations and parties to attend.

Two terrorists, disguised as maintenance personnel in standard blue coveralls, carrying toolboxes with phony identification badges, reported to the control console chief to do routine meter calibrations.

On this particular night, console personnel were in good spirits after having been to the customary pizza and beer party before the holiday, and not many of the staff on the 2nd shift were overly attentive to their duties. Besides, these new facilities were so well safety interlocked in combination with annunciators to continuously display system status that any component failure or emergency would immediately trip a warning signal.

The two impostors are authorized to go ahead with no questions asked. So far, they have been successful in gaining access to the back of the console where the critical wire harnesses terminate on contact boards for easy servicing when performing preventative maintenance procedures.

The plan was to tamper with signals from sensors continuously monitoring reactor performance while it was operating at peak power. If these signals can be jammed at a constant normal and safe level of output, the reactor would undergo a runaway condition leading to a meltdown similar to the 1998 Chernobyl accident in the USSR. This would have a devastating effect on the densely populated northeastern sector of the United States. Casualties, no doubt, would be numbered in the hundreds of thousands, contamination becoming widespread while emergency crews would fight to bring the disaster under control. Cities such as New York and Boston could become uninhabitable for years to come because of the long-term presence of deadly nuclear radiation.

One of the terrorists has had a good amount of experience with power generating nuclear plants. Even though his technical expertise in the field is about five years behind present technology, he was a qualified technician with enough confidence to attempt the execution of such a fiendish scheme. He had terminated his association with the power industry because of his objectionable views on the nuclear industry.

He was a White extremist who had succumbed as a mercenary in the terrorist organization paying him a lucrative amount of money for his contribution to their cause.

The two had no trouble identifying the color-coded wires from the sensors that measured the temperature of the cooling water in the reactor. They proceeded to wire in a substitute constant level signal, which indicated a safe temperature level.

The system was now running with no actual temperature feedback from the reactor, and it would stray into an unsafe temperature region, undetected. It should be only a matter of a few minutes before the runaway condition overtook an irreversible meltdown from an excessively high reactor temperature developing. An explosion would quickly follow, as containment of the reactor would no longer be possible.

Having completed their mission, the two terrorists signed out at the control console and hurriedly exited the plant, now a virtual time bomb.

What the self-proclaimed expert technician was not aware of were the latest safeguards built into the systems in recent years. Backup redundant systems with self-checking capability could detect malfunctions almost as quickly as they occurred, thereby preventing dangerous levels of operation and providing warning alarms.

The two men had not yet reached the exit gate when the alarm went off, signaling a possible sabotage attempt. They were trapped inside the fenced-in power plant facility. As the terrorists got frantic and opened fire on the two guards inside the gate post, they themselves ran into a barrage of gunfire. One of them, a Black man, got killed instantly; and the second man was mortally wounded and died minutes later.

The second potential major disaster within a week had been averted by a combination of modern technology and a good amount of luck. It may just be that the terrorists were not capable of undertaking sabotage operations of such complexity.

21

During the next three weeks, Ben was torn between his work at NASA, concern for Mary's rapidly approaching delivery, and trying to get into the holiday spirit with Christmas and New Year's practically here.

"It's so sad," said Mary, "that this is supposed to be the season of peace, but horrific events are reported every day. And after that catastrophe in that small Canadian town…it's making everyone I talk to feel so vulnerable."

"That's the thing about terrorism," Ben said, "makes you live in a constant state of fear and anticipation of the worst."

"It's horrible. Human life is so fragile to begin with; why should people be running scared not knowing if they might be the next target?"

"I'd like to hear some news that the authorities are on to who's behind it," Ben said. He'd been working at a feverish pace to complete the TREND program. It was ironic that some of his best work would be used for showing man's gradual disappearance.

"This latest incident at London's Heathrow air terminal is a real shocker," Ben said. "Just how insane can these maniacs be to try setting off a nuclear bomb in a public place with such a high population close by? I don't know how much longer these kinds of threat can go on."

Mary nodded in agreement. "I just read in the paper that worrying about potential disasters is taking a toll. Victims are either fatalities or people suffering psychological breakdowns brought on by fear of what may happen next."

On New Year's Eve, the TREND program was finally complete –fully debugged and ready for use. There was no celebration such as would take place in more normal times. Staff members were too exhausted to try test cases. Ben's team was content with the knowledge that the program worked and was on schedule, and they left for a brief respite with their families.

Ben dreaded going back to the NASA Center on the first working day of the new year because of his anticipation of bad news when the TREND program would finally be put through its paces.

His team of analysts and programmers, along with Fred Sherman and a few other senior managers, gathered at the computing laboratory to see a demonstration of what the TREND program could do.

Ben was the first one to address the group. "Colleagues, for the past three years, we have been developing an infrared system to detect and quantize human life over the entire surface of our planet. As we are all aware, NASA and the military have been accumulating infrared data from global emissions for a good many years."

"Isn't this data available from our NASA archives, Ben?" one of the senior managers interjected.

"That's right. In fact, we have used much of that data as our information source because it represents recent history.

"For our purpose in the TREND program, we only deal in relative changes, usually with only one set of camera data at a time, so we don't have to concern ourselves with compatibility of many cameras. I'm assuming that you are all up to speed with our protocol distributed to you last week."

The 10 by 6 foot projection on the wall in front of us will display a computer generated color map along with the population data.

"Population is displayed by clusters of bright white dots, each representing a fixed relative quantity of people. One of the dots in a cluster will have an increasing intensity with time to indicate that the population is growing. If population is increasing, that one dot will increase in brightness until it can join the existing cluster of bright dots, and a new dot will then form to replace it. A decreasing population will have a reverse effect and dots in the cluster will disappear one by one.

"Large clusters of dots will show up in urban areas while single dots will be scattered in rural sections.

"If I didn't mention it before, the map to be viewed is selectable. This means that we are not restricted to global mapping. We can also put a limit on viewing area by selecting individual countries or even sections of large countries.

"In the top right-hand corner of the projection, you'll see two number sets. The top one represents the total number of population dots on the map being observed. As the population changes up or down, so will that number. The number below that is the date shown by month, day of the month, and year the data was taken.

"Now that I'm all talked out, why don't we start some demonstration runs? Does anyone have a favorite part of the world to look at first?"

"Why don't we go to a global display first," Fred Sherman said, "and let's cover a time span from two years ago to the present. And then, we go from there."

After the room lights were dimmed and the program set up, a crisp map of the world appeared on the screen. A few seconds later, the computer spread bright dots over the map to signify people on Earth – two years ago. A dot count of several hundred lit up in the top right-hand corner of the map and the first date to appear was December of the year that just ended. The time scale was set at one minute of display time equal to fifteen days of real calendar time.

The data updated about once every 30 seconds and depicted an ever-increasing count, indicating that the global population was steadily climbing in that time period, as expected. In fact, the population increased right up to the present date.

"Let's repeat the test over the same time span, but this time, we can observe some of the major countries or even continents," someone called out.

The European continent was selected first. Starting two years ago, its population was also seen to climb steadily right up until September.

Then, it slowed to a standstill and remained constant until December. The last two updates showed a count that began to decrease.

Not a sound was heard in the room for a couple of minutes except for the circulating fans churning away to keep the computers in the room from overheating. Everyone realized that they were witnessing definite proof that White race population had begun a downward trend.

Finally, someone else in the room said, "Let's check a few more areas like North America and the Far East and Africa."

North America showed the same trend as Europe, but the Far East and even Africa showed a continuing increase. The TREND program obviously worked well, but there was no applause for a job well done. Everyone in the room seemed in a somber mood.

As a last test in the shakedown testing of TREND, Fred Sherman had a somewhat morbid suggestion. "Why don't we look at the western part of North America using the oldest infrared data that we have?"

The earliest recorded data going back to 1961 was used as a source and the program was started. Data updates were set for one per year, every 30 seconds; then for the last two years, the updates at 30-second intervals would be for fifteen-day increments.

The Northwestern states and the Canadian provinces of British Columbia and Alberta were depicted first in lively colors on the screen. This was followed by clusters of bright white dots in inhabited areas. Attention naturally was drawn to the few large cities, both American and Canadian, which seemed to hoard most of the population.

The rest of the land was sparsely populated as evidenced by widely separated white dots.

As time went on, the total count was shown to increase steadily, indicating a rising population. Then in 1964, a white dot popped up and intensified about a hundred or so miles east of Edmonton, Alberta.

Everyone present was quick to grasp what was happening: *the small town of Munroe had been established!* A sense of awe was palpable in the room.

Time marched on. Munroe eventually grew into a two-dot town where it seemed to reach a plateau.

Moving into the time period of the prior year, the data updates were sped up, but Munroe held at a two-dot town. Then it happened. On the December 15th update, the double dots disappeared completely. *The inhabitants of Munroe had been slaughtered by poison gas on December 12th. There were no survivors.*

No one had a word to say. They left the room deep in thought. They had witnessed the birth and the demise of a populated area on the Earth's surface during recent history, a direct result of an insane act by mankind.

22

JANUARY

On January 14th, Ben Davidson headed for the Houston Medical Center for his one year checkup with Dr. Robert Armstrong. The past year had been an eventful one for him and his wife. Between his own heart transplant surgery, his work at the NASA Space Center, and Mary's pregnancy, the two of them had managed to survive some hectic times.

He should be happy with his recent accomplishments at the Space Center, but instead, he feels like he has signed mankind's death warrant. There was no doubt about the turndown in the population of the White race and most likely the rest of mankind will be subject to the same fate. If Mary and he were to be blessed with children, what kind of future was in store for them?

Dr. Armstrong greeted him with a firm handshake and a friendly smile. "You sure are a picture of health, Ben. What have you been doing with yourself to look so fit?" He was obviously pleased with Ben's physical appearance.

"I feel great, Doc. I took up jogging a couple of months ago along with my once a week tennis at the racket club; it has really put me back into shape."

"How's Mary doing? The two of you must be getting anxious by now. You said she was expecting around February 6th – that's a few weeks from now."

"Yep, she's due about that time and so far – no complications. We're having a girl."

Dr. Armstrong had a quizzical expression on his face; he couldn't help wondering if other White families would ever conceive again.

"Let's get you checked over, Ben. Then I'd like to talk to you about something else."

During the next half hour, Ben got a thorough physical exam, with special attention to his heart. Dr. Armstrong finished the exam by taking a blood sample which he handed over to the attending nurse with instructions for an immediate blood count to be done at the lab.

"If your white corpuscles are at a normal level, I would say that you passed this year's exam with flying colors, Ben. It looks like you've adapted to your new heart very well. In fact, if I had not done the transplant surgery myself, I'd never believe it possible that you have someone else's heart inside of you. Like I've said before, I am still amazed that there has never been any sign of rejection whatsoever."

"Doc, I'd like to be candid with you for a minute. My fantastic recovery doesn't seem right. I've never needed anti rejection drugs, and from what little I know about these things – that is unheard of.

"Not that I'm not thankful for what's happened, but I'm not a believer in miracles. There is something mighty strange going on – wouldn't you agree?"

Ben was expressing concern about his own condition, but also thinking about other recent world events, equally mind boggling.

"Perceptive observation, Ben. Of course I agree. Whatever is happening appears to be well beyond our medical comprehension. Completely uncomplicated organ transplants such as your own, total remission from terminal illness, infertility. You have to wonder what's in store for the White race on this planet."

"It's almost like we are in a state of suspended animation," Ben added.

"As if we didn't have enough problems, that idiot Fieldstone, has really done a job stirring up racial prejudice in the world. It seemed like every time he opened his mouth he was raising the world tensions another notch. It was a mistake to open up our files to his partner,

Coleman, back a few months ago. Now the damage has been done and the White race is at the mercy of those imbalanced terrorists.

"You know, Ben, we have become an endangered species."

"It's like the nonwhite extremists have a vendetta against us which was waiting all these years to be triggered – and now it won't quit. It shouldn't be surprising when you look back and realize the conquests and atrocities that those people have suffered at the hands of the White race."

"Gradual demise is not the term for it, Ben. Do you realize the White race has got about one generation to go before it becomes too late to survive as a race? We should thank God that you and Mary are denying this unexplainable phenomenon, but you and a few others like you would not be nearly enough to preserve our race. Unless we do something to overcome this sudden widespread sterility among White people, we will become extinct."

"Is there a chance, Doc, that what we are suffering from is a viral disease? There must be a good amount of research going on in medical labs trying to find a cure for it."

"If it is a virus-type of infection, there is a good chance that it is contagious, Ben. Then it's only a matter of time before it spreads to the other races in the world."

"Is it possible that the problem is environmental? Look at the atmospheric pollution we've produced over the years. We know that acid rain, for example, has killed plant life in many areas on Earth. In fact, aren't there many species of marine life that have disappeared because of polluted water supplies? Why couldn't humans be subject to the same fate?"

"These are very definite possibilities, Ben. However, don't you think there may be a fundamental connection between the sterility problem and the spectacular recoveries in medicine that we've experienced in the past year?

"All of these things have been time coincidental – that's what is so baffling to the imagination. I somehow think that you put your finger on it a few minutes ago when you mentioned being in a state of suspended animation."

"The problem could be genetic. Is that what you are alluding to, Doc?"

"At this point we can't rule out any possible cause for the problem. Actually, as of right now nobody in the medical profession has any idea what brought on such a condition. What is important is that we don't waste any more time before we try to do something about it."

"That may cover a pretty wide territory," Ben said. "The answer may be like the old needle in a haystack, but I agree with you, Doc. It may take a monumental effort on the part of the scientific community to solve the puzzle – and hopefully come up with a reasonable solution."

"Which brings us to what I wanted to talk to you about, Ben. How would you like to attend a meeting with me on this subject in Washington, DC, two weeks from today?"

"Sure – but what kind of contribution would I be expected to make?"

"Don't be so modest, Ben. What you've told me about your infrared work in demography fits right in with the subject matter we'll be discussing at our meeting with the president."

"What's that got to do with the immediate problem of restoring the White race's fertility so he can procreate again? Besides, I don't have any words of wisdom for the president."

A knock on the door drew their attention to the nurse who stuck her head inside. "Pardon me for interrupting, Dr. Armstrong, but I have the lab report on Mr. Davidson's blood test." The nurse handed him the computer printout.

"Thank you, Judy." He checked the results.

"The white count is exactly where it should be. There's no doubt about it – your system is adapting very nicely to its new heart. My prognosis is that you should live to a very ripe old age."

The two men were obviously pleased at the report – but not surprised.

"Now back to our original discussion," Dr. Armstrong continued. "I've asked about twenty-five experts in the scientific community to meet in Washington. Our objective is to get across a mood of urgency while also recommending an immediate course of action concerning the present global problem facing a large portion of the population. It's important that we impress upon him the unavoidable fate of extinction for the entire human race, unless we do something about it right now."

"Are you talking about experts in the medical field – because isn't that where a crash effort is really needed?" Ben cut in.

"Not necessarily so. Nobody knows what the cause of this zero birth rate might be. The problem could have a fundamental nature to it, such as living conditions on Earth no longer being suitable to support the conception of human life itself – perhaps those of us belonging to the White race are more sensitive to it, but there's a strong likelihood that nonwhites will be the next to suffer the same fate – scientifically speaking, there's not much that differentiates races from each other.

"In reality, we have a maximum of forty years or so to find a solution – if our race is to survive on this planet. Your demographic studies would support that premise, wouldn't they, Ben?"

"When you put it that way, I guess you're right, Doc – it's important that we investigate every branch of science in a parallel effort so as not to waste time. We are caught up in a race against time where each year that goes by without a solution will mean a two or so percent drop in the White population based on today's numbers."

"That's why I'm asking you to attend the meeting. Believe me, you won't be the only representative from the physical sciences. The backgrounds of the attendees will cover the gamut from the entire medical field, to the physical and social sciences, and then some. You should feel quite at home with your kind of scientists from MIT, Princeton, Stanford, Livermore Labs, Los Alamos, to name a few.

"I've also invited Charley Stafford and Louis Keck from the Fusion Lab at Southwestern Tech in Austin. This guy, Keck, has done some theoretical work in physics that may fit right in with our subject matter.

"So what do you say, Ben? Can I count on you to attend?"

"Of course you can count me in. I feel honored to be invited to a gathering of such a prestigious group. Thanks for asking me."

"Good; I'd like you to participate in the planning session by presenting some of your recent results. I'm sure others present will be making a pitch for more government funding in their own areas of interest. Hopefully, in a couple of days, we will have put together a multi-pronged plan of attack covering agreed upon areas worthy of further investigation. The next step will be to meet with the president at the oval office to present him with the facts – as well as we know them. Our objective is to get federal funding as soon as possible to get these projects underway."

"You said two weeks from today. Is that for the planning session or the meeting with the president?"

"I'd like you to be at the first meeting which will last two days. Our appointment with the President is scheduled for 9:00 am, the day after the planning session, on January 31st. That meeting will be limited to four people, including myself. We don't want to overwhelm the poor guy with this monumental problem. I trust you won't have any problem with your own management fitting this into your schedule. And you should be back home in plenty of time for the big event with Mary."

"I won't have any problem at the Space center. They like the visibility, any time there's an opportunity. That's part of our job. I'm more concerned with Mary's situation, although we don't anticipate any problems. I'll be there on the 29th and I'm looking forward to it."

The two of them shook hands and Ben headed back to work at the Space Center, pleased with his own favorable status report and then – his surprise invitation to the Washington meeting.

23

Various attitudes among White people surfaced. They ranged from a willingness to fight for survival, to hopelessness and despair, to acceptance of recent events as the Will of God.

Finally, a mounting resistance to stop the two-pronged process of attrition to eliminate the White race rapidly developed. The matter of terrorist activities was being investigated worldwide by security organizations, with an intensified focus on cutting off their source of supply for the grotesque weapons of destruction they had been using.

Chemical weapons, outlawed by the Geneva Convention many years ago as inhumane in warfare, were still stockpiled by many peace-loving countries as a deterrent to their use. Black market operations had in turn been able to procure these same weapons from willing profiteers to supply the terrorists.

The countries that had been storing these weapons, quickly agreed, via UN legislation, to destroy their existing supplies and dismantle the manufacturing facilities for producing them. Those countries known to be resisting this new edict were delivered ultimatums to conform or else their own weapons, arsenals, and manufacturing facilities would be bombed to destruction.

Some countries chose to be mavericks, and ignored the UN proclamation. In those few cases, joint operations by military forces from countries designated by the UN swiftly carried out raids to wipe out supplies and facilities.

The use of nuclear weapons by the terrorists posed an even bigger problem. The failure of the first attempt to use a plutonium bomb as a weapon for large-scale destruction of human life was by no means, an indication that they would not try again. It terrified many who didn't doubt that the terrorists had technically qualified personnel within their organization able to make the next try a successful one, reeking devastating loss of life and contamination. What had been feared as a possibility during the years of the cold war could become a reality. There appeared to be no limit to the atrocious crimes against humanity the terrorists would resort to.

Again, the answer to the problem lay in the destruction of all nuclear weapons worldwide, to eliminate their possible procurement by the black market for resale to the terrorists. Since there were relatively few countries with nuclear capability, it didn't take long to reach an accord to destroy all existing atomic warheads and to halt further assembly of such weapons.

The agreement would not have been possible in times of rigid political differences between major powers in the world. However, the great changes toward democratic rule with associated greater personal freedoms in countries once under Communistic rule, had supported progressive diplomacy, and survival and the cessation of barbaric behavior unified everyone.

The implementation of the plan to rid the world of deadly weapons could not be accomplished overnight. Accordingly, a time limit of six months from January 15, was set for the total elimination of chemical weapons. In addition, nuclear weapons were to be destroyed, starting immediately and by July 15th, two years later, all such weapons were to have been dismantled, with no possibility of future use. The plutonium and uranium 235 were to be salvaged and palletized for safe storage in sub-critical amounts for later use in peaceful power generation applications.

So much for putting a lid on terrorist activities, but what about the inability of the White race to replicate itself? Was this only a temporary situation, or a long lasting problem with a corrective solution not yet in sight?

The last White infants to be born (up to the middle of October), would grow to adulthood in eighteen or so years. From that time on until the age of forty-five, give or take a couple of years, they should be biologically capable of reproducing. Unless fertilization could be restored during the time interval between now and forty-five years from now, the White race as a component of the human race would become extinct.

Those prone to dramatics espoused that humanity could well be entering a terminal phase on the planet and should start thinking about starting anew in the world of the hereafter. "Recent world events have been signaling the beginning of the end," they proclaimed, "and the White race, in particular, better brace itself for the worst."

For the people who could not face the growing fear of becoming extinct, the past year had been full of messages spelling doom for life on Earth. Their pessimistic outlook was one of hopelessness. Their cry was, "Nature has decided that man, as a living creature on this planet, has been too greedy and is no longer desirable. He has been wastefully consuming natural resources to satisfy his own selfish needs. Therefore, the time has come to do away with humankind before it destroys an environment that can still support other life forms on Earth." Many of those people became despondent and chose the faster way out, by taking their own lives.

The recent suicide rate throughout the world showed a stepped up increase of over three hundred percent with signs the upward surge would continue.

As is often the case in times of crisis and uncertainty, attendance at houses of worship showed a dramatic increase. People flocked to churches as the only recourse left for spiritual comfort. "Whatever destiny is facing man, it is Nature's way of enforcing the Will of God. Man must accept the inevitable and prepare to meet his Maker," was that group's mantra. Religious services in churches and synagogues throughout the Western world stepped up to handle record growth in demand. Dwindling attendances of the past reversed, and people of all ages swarmed to religious worship. Religion once again became a major contributor to the quality of life and a preparation for the hereafter.

And what would the world do without its optimists? Another large block of people believed a miracle would happen and were willing to bide their time until the problem eventually went away. Some among this group had faith in the creativity and intelligence of scientists, while others, the entitled, forever took the comforts of life for granted. They had been protected from world suffering by their wealth and status and didn't concern themselves with concerns like man's abuse of nature, the environment, or of their fellow inhabitants.

Of course there were others who seized on the dire circumstances by inventing money-making schemes. As was typical, they took advantage of their fellowmen who were tormented by a very real problem.

24

Early on the morning of January 29th, Ben Davidson and his wife shared a quick cup of coffee before Ben left Galveston to board the 6:30 Delta flight from Houston to Washington.

"I'll be back here Tuesday night, Hon. So try to keep a low profile and take it easy while I'm at the meeting."

"Don't you worry about a thing, Dear. Kristin and I will be just fine. It's time for you to head for the airport or you'll miss your plane. Bye now – and have a good trip."

The two of them hugged and kissed. Then Ben left to catch his flight. He was quite concerned about Mary's condition and almost felt guilty about not being at her side, especially at a time like this. Her doctor had assured the two of them that the baby should go full term, but there was always a slim chance that she would deliver early. Ben dreaded the thought of not being there for the big event.

The flight to Washington was uneventful and arrived on time. After checking in at the Shoreham, Ben headed for the meeting room at the hotel in time to hear Dr. Armstrong's opening remarks since he was chairing the planning session.

"Ladies and Gentlemen, I'm glad to see you all made it here on time so let's get down to the business at hand. I only wish our get together were under more pleasant circumstances.

"The day of reckoning for the White race on this planet appears to have arrived as I'm sure many of you have realized. The events of the past year have left us all in a state of shock. First we were deceived by a feeling of euphoria over our apparent great success in medicine. More recently, we have undergone a complete reversal to a mood of total despair over the sudden realization of our zero birth rate. These disparate biological occurrences have had serious repercussions, as ongoing acts of terrorism attest to.

"Might there be a link between these events? That is why we are gathered here today. We must come up with a plan of action which will lead to some answers before it's too late. Whether we like it or not, we are engaged in a race against time to restore the White race's ability to reproduce. Unless we come up with a solution sometime within the next forty or so years, we will become extinct as a race."

Bob Armstrong paused at this point to look about the conference room for a reaction from the audience.

"Aren't we faced with a medical problem here, Doctor?" Charley Stafford remarked while there was quiet in the room. "How come so many of us who were invited to this meeting are from fields outside of medicine?"

"Actually, Professor Stafford, we are faced with a phenomenon that nobody understands at the moment. It's like nothing we have ever experienced before. My good friend, Ben Davidson, from NASA, suggested that our predicament may be one of suspended animation. If so, what does that mean? Is it possible we are faced with only a temporary situation that will correct itself in due time – or might we be destined to remain in such a state indefinitely?

"A few minutes ago, Tom Curtis, one of our foremost experts in the field of pathology and more recently in genetic medicine, put it to me from a different point of view. It may be that White man's biological clock has come to a stop. How can we restart it?

"We cannot ignore the possibility that a virus is at the root of the problem. If so, will it prove to be contagious? How much time do the other races on Earth have before they are also stricken with the fertility problem?

"Then again, our problem may be one of not being able to cope with an environment that has become too toxic. It may be that our form of life can no longer survive under present conditions on Earth. But why only the White race?

"Isn't the White race's newly discovered stamina in resisting deadly diseases and yet apparent sterility in direct conflict with each other? We do know the onset of these two anomalies occurred at about the same time. Could they be related?

"Last but not least, can knowledge gained about the precipitating circumstances bring a stop to the ongoing persecution of the White race by terrorists?

"There you have it, ladies and gentlemen. I've posed several questions which may have answers in any one of the diverse areas of expertise present in this room today.

"Our immediate task is to formulate a plan whereby a number of research investigations can be carried out simultaneously; this will be absolutely necessary because of the time constraint we are faced with.

"The next step is to meet with the president the day after tomorrow to bring him up to speed with what is discussed at this meeting. Our recommended plan will require immediate funding to get it underway posthaste."

The meeting proceeded quickly with useful input from all branches of science represented. The consensus was that any ideas which looked promising must not be overlooked.

How to deal with impostors like Fieldstone and company who masqueraded as experts was also discussed. Those individuals had to be identified from their shallow set of credentials when they made their pitch for research funding to participate in this emergency effort. They must be barred from performing any "think-tank studies" that promised spectacular results with vague approaches to their methods.

Due to the gravity of the crisis and the increasing frequency of terrorist acts, there was consensus to recommend to the president that he make an appeal to citizens of all nations to please temper their emotions, as the very existence of life on Earth was being threatened.

Significant progress was made as the meeting went on late into the night, avenues of investigation selected. The agenda for the second day was to prioritize specific areas of inquiry and identify which studies or projects should start immediately. The rough dollar figures were estimated so that the president could be given a realistic appraisal of the funding necessary to carry out the emergency program.

At the top of the list of recommended programs was a massive effort in genetic medicine with parallel programs in genetic engineering to cover the possibility of gene alteration should that become necessary. The team would reach out to medical institutions across the world to access the latest knowledge in the field. Specialists with reputations of significant contributions to the advancement of medical science were singled out to launch their own programs. Among this group was Tom Curtis, who would assemble a team to address the characterization of the many human races with the goal of finding genetic differences between them. If differences in reproductive genes were found, then the necessary gene splicing to reactivate the White race would be turned over to genetic engineering experts.

The second prioritized research endeavor would be carried out in the field of viral medicine – jointly by research laboratories specializing in the field and by pharmaceutical houses. The goal was to identify a possible virus as the cause of the White race's sudden sterility and to develop an antitoxin to rid mankind of its destructive interference with procreation.

Environmental sciences would initiate programs to determine if humanity's recent technological advances and continued dependence on fossil fuels were fostering a detrimental impact on its ability to survive a changing environment. This scientific discipline had been a strong proponent of efforts to clean up the environment and study health hazards produced by pollution. For many years its warnings of impending disaster had been largely ignored, but now could be the time to convince nations of the world (especially the United States), that an environmental cleanup was long overdue.

The vulnerability of humankind to climatic changes, effecting chemical changes in the atmosphere, water supplies, and on the ground had been known for some time. It could be that man had gone a step too far in upsetting Nature's balance and drastic measures were required to reverse the process of extinction of life on Earth now underway. Close monitoring of human pollution on a global basis was deemed imperative.

Additionally, the science of demography was vital, not only in identifying changes in pollution concentrations, but it could well become a diagnostic tool to locate uninhabitable places on the Earth's surface. It would be extremely useful in providing a measure of humanity's response to whatever breakthroughs would be achieved by science to reverse the decreasing population trend. Ben Davidson's infrared research would continue at an accelerated pace.

On a grander scale, the chance that the present dire dilemma was caused by some fundamental physical change taking place on Earth, as a planet in the solar system, or even in the universe itself, could not be overlooked.

The evolutionary processes through the ages of life, both animal and plant, have been greatly influenced by the environment. It can be argued that humans, themselves, are products of their environment. Perhaps a physical change has come along to pose a threat to life as we know it, and our survival may be in jeopardy because of our inability to adapt to this change. Man's own destiny may be beyond his control.

Nevertheless, the physics of the universe must be continuously researched as there are still many facets of it that we know nothing about. Research programs like the one at Southwestern Institute in Austin, would be extended to include a modeling study of the Big Bang theory. Louis Keck would be provided immediate funding to continue his work on the project.

It was unanimously agreed that constant monitoring of the research activities must be done in order to keep all participants on track and to guide them along during the course of their programs. Funding must be made available for scientists to participate in frequent seminars where progress on their individual programs would be under constant scrutiny.

A review panel would be appointed to pass judgment on programs as they developed. The modus operandi was created to produce a constant flow of up-to-date information whose merits could be evaluated rapidly. Promising areas of research would be rewarded with increased funding to speed up progress while projects floundering aimlessly would be terminated.

The second day's session was nearly over when Ben Davidson is paged to answer an urgent telephone call from Galveston Hospital in Texas.

"Hi – Ben? Krissy couldn't wait any longer – she arrived forty-five minutes ago at six pounds six ounces."

"Is everything alright, Hon? I'm so sorry I wasn't there with you. I'll head home on the 5:30 flight and I should arrive at 8:00. There were no complications, I hope."

"Don't you worry about a thing, Dear. Mother and daughter are both doing fine. I went into labor late this morning, and Dr. Price thought it best if I checked into the hospital right away. Cathy, next door, drove me in and everything went fine.

"We have ourselves a little doll – I'm so anxious for you to see how precious she is."

"Sit tight, Hon, and I'll be there before you know it. Goodbye for now."

Upon Ben's return to the meeting room, Bob Armstrong inquired about Mary's condition, positive that's what the telephone call was about.

"She's doing great – and so is our baby girl," Ben said, smiling.

"A beam of good news," Bob said. "Mind if I share it with the group?"

"No, not at all, and I've got to run. Best of luck with the president tomorrow."

"Wave goodbye to the new dad, everybody," Bob said to the group as Ben gathered up his papers and headed for the door. "One of the exceptions to the rule, Ben and his wife are the proud parents of their first child, a daughter."

Whoops, cheers, and surprised looks were the response to Bob's announcement.

Dr. Theresa Winters, one of the physicists, whispered to the colleague sitting next to her, "I bet they'll be testing her genes soon."

"Hopefully this happy event in Ben Davidson's life is an omen of what's in store for all of us in future years. Thank you all for the contributions you have made during the past two days to help launch our emergency program. We'll be in touch with you after tomorrow's meeting with the president. Thanks again."

At a few minutes before 9:00AM the next day, Bob Armstrong, Tom Curtis, Erik Stevens and Charley Stafford were escorted to a small room at the White House by a staff member to await their appointed time with the President of the United States.

"The president has already met with three other groups this morning – so you can appreciate the busy schedule he has," the staffer said, briefing them on White House protocol.

At precisely 9:00 o'clock the signal light in the hallway flashed, indicating the president was ready, and the four visitors were led into the Oval Office.

After introductions and the customary handshakes, the president beckoned the four men to take seats in the visitors' chairs laid out closely around the front of his desk while he sat at the helm in the Commander in Chief's chair. This was a first time experience for the four men and each one felt awed at the thought of visiting the President of the United States in the Oval Office.

"Gentlemen, I read your emailed proposal last night and was impressed with the scope of scientific inquiry and your team's level of expertise. Your reputations precede you," the president said, wasting no further time with small talk.

"Mr. President, we have a grace period of forty some years, after which time infants of today will approach menopause and consequently lose their ability to reproduce."

"Dr. Armstrong, this is exactly what I was advised about three days ago by the Central Intelligence Agency and the Office of the Surgeon General. You've confirmed the serious nature of our predicament.

"I agree with your committees' assessment, Gentlemen: that a multi-disciplinary approach is warranted and expediency is paramount. You have my wholehearted support. The National Science Foundation will act as a clearing house for allocation of funding. I saw that you have built in reviews and checks on the various projects, and trust that the money will be spent wisely."

"Mr. President, we appreciate your support and you can rest assured that we plan to watchdog our activities on a constant basis to avoid squandering tax payer's money or vital time," Bob Armstrong replied.

"Now sir," Bob continued, "we do not mean to be out of line, but suggestions also arose in relation to the continuing acts of terrorism occurring around the world.

"We hope you will consider making a worldwide appeal to all nations for their support during this critical period in history. Those responsible for committing acts of terrorism, especially, should reconsider their motives because they may well be risking their own futures by their present evil actions."

"That, Dr. Armstrong, is already in the works. I'll be taking part in a joint appeal with the leaders of member countries of the United Nations, to do exactly what you are suggesting. The appeal is to be aired worldwide next Monday."

"Thank you, Mr. President," each of the visitors said.

The president rose. "I wish you Godspeed in your mission and will be anxiously following your progress. I feel hopeful that the collective of bright minds in your group will find answers in time to offset a possible catastrophe."

"Thank you again, Mr. President, that is our great hope as well," said Bob Armstrong, and they left one step closer to doing just that.

25

FEBRUARY

Four days after the White House meeting to set up the emergency program to save mankind, the President of the United States and the heads of state from Russia, Great Britain, France, Germany, Japan, India, the Middle East, China, and other countries too numerous to mention, met with the United Nations General Assembly in New York to present a unified appeal to all nations of the world for cooperation. Each head of state delivered an address in his native language for radio and television coverage worldwide stressing the importance of working together to seek answers to the biological problems facing the world, a cessation to the terrorist response, and the vital need to pull together for a common cause.

The speeches, worded so as not to antagonize members of the terrorist organization, were beamed to all nations in the world via the Voice of America, the BBC, Radio Moscow, and the Far East radio and television networks in appropriate languages. The broadcasting was repeated continually for a period of seventy-two hours to make sure that everybody on the surface of the Earth was aware of the struggle for survival humankind was currently engaged in.

One last murder was committed. Luke Fieldstone was given the same treatment as the Klansmen in the Magnolia Massacre. On the night of February 10th, a policeman cruising his beat near the Capitol in Washington, DC, found Luke's body hanging from a tree limb,

In general however, the response to the worldwide broadcasts was almost miraculous. Within a week, evidence of persecution of the White race disappeared. What had been daily reporting of cruel murders of White victims in a holocaust to exterminate them suddenly came to a complete stop. The search for the identity of the guilty ones quietly proceeded behind the scenes, but reporting on that was hushed up.

In the meantime, the United States led the offensive to save humankind. Scientists of all races in every nation worked against the clock to find a solution to unlock the secret of procreation, because it was assumed inevitable that people, regardless of race, could become afflicted in the same way in the not too distant future.

Tom Curtis had been assigned the task of leading a team of experts in the field of genetics in a gene characterization program. Their goal was to identify differences in the gene structures by race. The effort involved studies of the DNA molecule in an attempt to uncover unique racial characteristics that had not been sought before.

Tom was still undecided on how to proceed. He was the type of person who needed to motivate himself with a logical, results-oriented plan. He knew what the ultimate goals were, but was a pragmatic individual who realized success would most likely come in small, meaningful steps, each contributing to the final answer.

It was almost two months into the program, but Tom was still probing for a plan of attack. He'd come up with a line of inquiry, brainstormed on it with his group, but so far, all had exhibited dead-ends. Usually, this was a stimulating part of the scientific process, however, not when under this much time pressure.

One afternoon, he was in his office at the school, mentally reviewing a simple experiment he'd been considering, when Molly came in from the lab to see how he was doing.

"You sure are in deep thought, Dear. I hope I didn't distract you," said Molly almost apologetically.

"No problem, Moll. I've been kicking around this idea about an easy test that could help launch our gene characterization program. Want me to tell you about it?"

Molly could sense when her husband was onto some new idea. "Go ahead. Use me as a sounding board if you like."

"I plan to run a test in in-vitro fertilization using subjects from the student body here at the college."

"Sounds interesting enough, but I don't see the connection with your genetics research program."

"OK – well listen to this. First we'll need volunteers to participate in this experiment. The test will involve a male and a female from each of three races – White, Black, and Asian.

"Next I want to set up a test matrix in which there are nine possible mating combinations. You know what I mean, don't you?"

"I think so. You're talking about White with White, White with Black, White with Asian, and so on, aren't you?"

"That's exactly right. If you think about it for a minute, there are nine combinations when you take into account the male and female factor. We need six healthy students where the three females are willing to provide us with eggs at ovulation time and the males will furnish sperm for the invitro fertilization."

"It's an interesting experiment, Dear. Why don't you go ahead with it?"

"I will as soon as I get authorization from the school officials. When I tell them the purpose of the test, I'm sure they'll grant me permission. We have to start somewhere – and setting up this benchmark could explain why reproduction among mixed races is still apparently flourishing."

Permission was granted and six volunteers were screened for the tests which were performed at the school medical clinic and the genetics laboratory.

Tom Curtis was not surprised with the results, but now he had established a basis for a genetic connection to the reproduction dilemma of the White race. Successful fertilization was demonstrated in a laboratory dish while viewed under a microscope for all combinations except – White with White.

Tom's findings were reported at the first review seminar as clinical proof of the purebred White sterility problem. The cause of the problem seemed to lie in some genetic quirk residing only in members of the White race or it could be a secret of Nature that was yet to be understood.

There was unanimous agreement at the meeting that a stepped up effort in researching man's genetics was warranted immediately; Tom Curtis was requested to move his activity to the National Laboratory for Genetics Research in San Diego.

During this same period, Louis Keck was engaged in planning a program to simulate the Big Bang. The problems being experienced in the world appeared so fundamental that even a look at this aspect of our origin was not considered too far fetched.

Lou was at a loss about what role he could play in the great scientific effort.

"You sure did quite a selling job promoting my simulation of the fusion process at the Washington meeting," Lou said to Charley Stafford during one of their frequent brainstorming sessions . "I'm having difficulty relating my kind of expertise to all the medical talent now working on this project."

"You're much too conservative, Lou. The simulation work you've done in the short time since you came here has given us a new slant on the fusion process. At the time you were doing this work, you were leaving the door open for possible application to the Big Bang itself, remember?"

"Yes I know, Charley, that was so I could work out a generalized solution with no constraints on it. I'm not so sure we can turn this thing around to also follow the effects of the Big Bang after the fact. I'm talking about the expanding universe."

"Why not? The mechanics of that process is like a response to an impulse. The fusion reaction itself is what provided the impulse and the debris of the explosion with a lot of momentum outward is our expanding universe.

"So far you've only looked at the shape of the impulse – and you've done a commendable job on that. Now – what's wrong with carrying that one step further to see how that expansion progresses with time?"

"I see what you're saying, Charley. It's just that I fail to see this project as a very high priority item when compared to the problems facing the medical experts right now."

"You know darn well that everyone at the Washington meeting was groping for possible areas in science worthy of further investigation. Your project stirred up a good amount of interest. You see, Lou – no one has any positive ideas at this point. It's anybody's guess where the answers might be."

"Don't get me wrong, Charley. I welcome the opportunity to work on a project as interesting at this one. It's the kind of research I've always wanted to do, but I could never get a sponsor to finance the effort. Now it seems I have "carte blanche" to try anything I want to. You realize, of course, that there are no guarantees in this game."

"Don't worry about that, Lou. All anyone can ask is that you give it your best effort. Come hell or high water, if anything good comes of it, we are that much farther ahead. If nothing positive happens, at least we know you gave it your best shot. That's the nature of research – right?"

"You know me – I've always had reservations about squandering the taxpayer's money."

"Only this time – if someone doesn't come up with answers, it won't make a darn bit of difference, will it? Let's think positive about the entire matter. We are better off not to keep reminding ourselves of the time left on the doomsday clock. Your original goal of determining the age of this universe of ours is a good area to concentrate on. Who knows? You may uncover some surprises along the way. Keep up the good work, Lou." And the two of them finished their discussion.

In the meantime, Ben Davidson has returned to NASA Houston to continue his research in demography. Even though his efforts may not contribute directly to solving the sterility problem, his infrared technique of determining world population, practically on demand, would be extremely useful in monitoring world developments.

The CENSUS program had been completed and was nearly operational except for a few refinements needed to make it more user friendly.

The remaining task was to put the system on-line so it could produce up-to-date results of world population surveys. Up to now the basic system had been fed from historical records stored on magnetic tape which were suitable for debugging purposes and demonstration runs.

However, the real value of the computer program would be realized when it made its calculations almost in real time as data was downloaded to NASA Houston for receiving stations around the globe. The stations were in direct contact with the polar orbiting satellite when it was traveling over their respective receiving ranges.

Ben figured it would take another two months before the system was fully operational.

Krissy was four months old that day, and Ben hurried home for another of her frequent birthday celebrations. He and Mary had adapted well to parenthood; it was pure pleasure to watch their daughter change day by day as her own unique little personality emerged.

"How's our little bundle of joy doing today, Honey?" Ben said as Mary greeted him at the door with a big hug and kiss.

"She's such a good baby, Hon. I changed her diaper a few minutes ago and how she was talking to herself – can you hear her? She started doing this a couple days ago before she goes to sleep. I think her disposition is so good – I wonder who she takes after?"

"Must take after her mother. I can see her now, in twenty years – a social butterfly – just like you. You know – I think she's the kind of child who's going to need companionship. We can't have her talking to herself all the time."

"Funny you should say that, Ben. Brace yourself. I was at the doctor's this afternoon, and he told me I'm pregnant again. I am so happy – it's like I am walking on air. Can you imagine the two of us being blessed with another baby, especially at a time like this?"

Ben was obviously pleased, but the surprised expression on his face was also for another reason. "Yes, I'm happy too, Dear. It's just that I wonder how come you and I are being singled out to uphold the White race? Doesn't that seem strange to you? About all I can add is that I'm very thankful we're able to make up for the time lost during the long bout with my failing heart. Do you think that could have anything to do with it?"

That evening, Ben and Mary chatted about their new plans, now that their second baby was on the way. The phone rang and Mary answered it.

"It's for you, Hon. I think it's Dr. Armstrong."

"Hi Doc. What can I do for you tonight?"

"Sorry to bother you at this odd hour, Ben, but I'm in the middle of setting up an agenda for our next review seminar. I'd like you to give us an update on your infrared research at our meeting. Do you think we can meet at the NASA Lab for this one? As you know, there is a good amount of interest in your demographic studies, and if you could give us a full blown demonstration of the system in operation, it would be appreciated by everyone present."

Three seminars had taken place so far, each one at a different location, so this request was standard operating procedure. Meeting places were selected for convenience only and no particular part of the country favored. It was expected that host sites would range all over the United States and quite likely in other countries during the course of the intensive research program.

"Sure, Doc. That can be arranged with no problem. As I mentioned to you once before, NASA welcomes this sort of visibility.

"When are you scheduling the seminar?"

"In about three weeks, depending on the availability of your facilities. We've established a pattern of Monday meetings to take advantage of the preceding weekend for travel. Can you get back to me sometime tomorrow after you've talked to your management? Then we can set a definite date to notify attendees. Incidentally, pardon me for not asking sooner, but how are you all doing these days? Your own health is good, or else I would have heard from you. And Mary and the new baby are fine?"

"I'll get back to you on availability by tomorrow afternoon, Doc, but I don't anticipate any problem setting up a Monday meeting date. Now – the answer to your other questions. Yes, we are all feeling great – in fact, my dear wife, Mary, just announced that she is expecting a second baby in about eight months. This time around I'll make sure that I'm present for the big event."

"Congratulations are in order to both of you. This is good news, indeed – especially in these times. I've held you up long enough, Ben – I'm sure you and Mary have a lot to talk about. Please get back to me tomorrow. Bye now."

After he hung up, Bob Armstrong also was dumbfounded about Mary's surprise pregnancy. A new twist had been added to the dilemma of the White race.

On a more somber note, Jim Coleman and his faithful sidekick, Alex Steiner, had effectively been put out of circulation since Luke Fieldstone's gruesome murder back in February. The two of them had been keeping a low profile for fear of getting the same treatment as Luke.

In the relatively short span of time since his dismissal as vice president at CIC, Jim's career has nosedived to its present level, and he felt despondent. His career had been a story of blind ambition, deception, marginal competence and poor judgment. Unfortunately, the worst consequence of his self-serving mistakes was a wave of terrorism in the world for which mankind had paid dearly.

At first, proud of the power of his written words and morbidly fascinated with the effects of the Fieldstone Study, he'd kept a scrapbook of every talk they presented to White supremacists, and then each senseless act of terror across the globe. Now, he obsessively turned the pages, sinking deeper and deeper into remorse and guilt. Up to now, he had been reluctant to face the error of his ways, but then, characters like him seldom ever do. His conscience worked on him as he witnessed the helpless state that the world is in, ruminated on his part of ruining the lives of victims and their families.

One night, Jim Coleman took his own life by jumping off the Arlington Bridge into the Potomac River. He left a note which Alex Steiner found. "Forgive me," was all it said.

His personal anchor lost, so followed the mind of Alex Steiner. He was picked up by the police, mumbling incoherently, dirty and beaten.

Taken to the state psychiatric facility, he became one more causality of selfish ignorance.

26

APRIL

*W*here to start? Where to start? Louis Keck pondered the perplexing question.

What if the entire universe was born during that one instant in time when the Big Bang was ignited? Then maybe it snuffed itself out almost as quickly as containment could not be maintained. The outer shells would be composed of a greater proportion of light elements, because the reaction had been cut short. These were thrown out first with the biggest kick. They were followed progressively by shells containing a greater percentage of heavier elements, but with less of a kick outward. The process quickly came to a stop when the conditions for fusion ceased to exist. At that point in time, the heavy elements that were left at the center had absorbed a good amount of the energy for their own formation and there was none left to propel them outward from what is now the center of the universe. The center can be thought of as a huge black hole that is pulling constantly on all the products of the Big Bang which are racing away from it.

A knock at the door signaled that Charley had arrived for one of their frequent brainstorming sessions.

"You know, Charley, I've been thinking about transitioning from the impulse generated by the fusion process itself to the expansion that follows it. It may be that we have to treat the impulse and the resulting expansion as one problem because there is a considerable amount of overlap between the two."

"I see what you mean, Lou; but that doesn't pose a problem, does it? Why can't you make use of your concentric shell approach throughout the analysis? Why not let them start at the instant when fusion begins to take place?"

"Hell – it won't make much difference anyway because the fusion time, which has the same duration as the impulse time, is in the order of a trillionth of a trillionth of a second. It will be long gone before the expansion really gets underway – and that's still in process after twenty or so billion years."

"I understand all that," Lou said, "but we have to make some assumptions in order to derive a working model. Furthermore, the outcome of this program is not going to be a simulation of the Big Bang. It has to be a theoretical model based on our assumptions and backed with actual data."

"What kind of data are you talking about, Lou? The only kind I am aware of are celestial observations indicating the Red Shift which proves that the universe is expanding. Is that what you mean?"

"Exactly, Charley. Those observations are telling us something. It's a matter of plugging that information into our equation of motion to verify that what we are doing is right or wrong."

"I see nothing wrong with that approach. Actually, each one of those observations is like a beacon at some known distance from us saying that it was moving away from us at a certain speed so many years ago. Many stars observed over the years can give you that kind of information.

"I think you are making progress, Lou. Stay with it and I guarantee you something will come of it."

Meetings with Charley stimulated Lou's imagination and made him feel like he was gaining a little better insight on how to proceed each time they met.

It took about seven months of concentrated effort tossing about numerous ideas before Lou and his team of researchers finally settled on an approach.

He mulled things over. *If in fact creation started with the Big Bang, what we are observing today is the ongoing explosion that we call the expanding universe. No matter in what direction we look, the stars that we observe are moving away from us. The reason for this is that our vantage point here on Earth happens to be inside the explosion.*

The question is: how much debris is there? Put in a different way, what is the mass of the universe? If all of this mass originated as hydrogen at the time of the creation, then the energy released during the Big Bang should be a function of it.

The assumption is made that time started at the moment of the Big Bang.

The fusion reaction that took place most likely was not complete as we know from our own experience with the H Bomb. Containment for a long enough period of time to allow fusion to be total just was not possible. In the case of the Big Bang, initial containment was achieved by the presence of extremely large gravitational forces which compressed the hydrogen nuclei until ignition took place and the fusion into heavier elements began to avalanche.

The entire reaction took place in a split second, during which time transmutation from the lighter to the heavier elements resulted in the creation of all the elements known to man. There was such an abundance of energy for an instant that even the heavier elements, which need an absorption of energy for their formation, were also created. Energy combining with what?

The explosive force outward quickly overtook and surpassed the gravitational force while the fusion process was escalating uncontrollably. The resulting debris of the reaction was thrust outward in all directions to become the expanding universe. Much of the unreacted hydrogen that was heaved out in space became fuel for the creation of future stars.

The universe can be thought of as being in a coasting state. The momentum outward is always decreasing due to the ever present gravitational attraction back to the center of gravity where it all started.

The situation out in space is unique in that the universe is not a solid mass and it does not have a uniform density. The total mass of the universe is not known and how it is distributed is also not known.

This is where Lou had to come to grips with a sticky problem. He had to make some valid assumptions if he was to derive a workable expression to produce the equation of motion describing the expanding universe.

Okay, let's assume that all parts of the universe will ultimately come to a stop at exactly the same time. For this to hold true, the percent change in speed per unit time will have to be the same for all parts of the universe *at any given time. The mass distribution will have been fixed to produce the correct acceleration at each location within the volume of the universe.*

He worked out the necessary relationships between gravitational mass, distance, and velocity at any point in the universe to derive the equation of motion for that point as a function of time since the Big Bang. The gravitational mass would be the mass contained in a sphere whose center coincided with the center of the universe with a radius equal to the distance of that point from the center.

Yes! It's possible to derive an expression to represent the distance traveled since the Big Bang for any point within the universe. That expression will be in the form of an equation where distance traveled is a function of time, remaining velocity, percent of the universal mass exerting a pull on that point and the universal mass itself. The percent factor will be known for each point in space in order to satisfy the precondition that all parts of the universe will stop expanding at exactly the same time before starting their fall back towards the center where the Big Bang took place. (And who knows how many billions of years until that happens?)

At the end of the workday, Lou went home feeling a sense of relief that he and his associates had finally picked an approach to explain the behavior of the universe. It had been a tedious process of evaluating one idea after another during the past several months and always facing disappointment when each one was ruled out for a whole range of reasons, from flaws in the idea itself, to insufficient information, or too much complexity. The newest approach had at its disposal a wealth of data from many years of astronomical star sightings.

That night, Lou spent time on his sundeck for another of his frequent star gazing sessions. It was November, and the night sky crystal clear with hundreds of stars visible to the naked eye.

The brightest stars in the heavens, Sirius, had just risen out of the southeastern horizon. The constellation Orion, named after the Greek warrior, stood out majestically as the most beautiful of the constellations visible. The three stars aligned at its center with Alnilam in the middle represented Orion's belt and pointed directly at Sirius.

Stars had been used as navigation aids going back to the early days of the explorers. Once the key star like Sirius was identified, it was a simple matter to swing an arc heading north in the stellar sky. The next star on this arc was Procyon followed by the twin stars, Castor and Pollux; and finally at the end of the arc in the northern sky was Capella. Those were some of the stars Lou had made frequent use of during his days as an aerial navigator in the US Air Force.

Thinking back to his military service days, Lou pictured the night sky as a map composed of reference points that could be relied upon to provide a sense of direction. If all else failed, the stars were there to lead the way. The one hundred or so of the more prominent stars that he had learned about during his navigation training were embedded so permanently in his head that he would never forget them. He was amazed after all these years how he had almost instant recall, by name, of all these stars and their locations in the sky.

Lou's mission was now very different, but he'd once again make use of the stars to accomplish his goal of helping to find man's origin in history.

During the next phase of his project, Lou would use star sightings, thousands of light years from Earth. They'd serve as test points to provide velocity and distance data for calculating the mass of the universe and hopefully its age.

The next morning, Lou had another session with Charley to bring him up to date on the methodology to be used on the program.

"Sounds like a sensible approach, Lou, but how are you dealing with the fact that the Earth is not at the center of the universe? The distances you mention are all estimated from this planet and yet the calculations will be based elsewhere."

"You're right, Charley. From our vantage point on Earth, the data would be skewed enough to really foul up our calculations. We plan to calculate the location of the center from the nonlinear character of the Red Shift with distance as seen from here. That's already been done by astronomers, and although we know there are an infinite number of galaxies, we believe that energetic forces are relational within circumscribed systems. So we'll work off of the indication that the center of our own galaxy is the Milky Way.

"We'll repeat those calculations using the most recent star sightings to get us the exact coordinates of that center."

"Then what are you going to do with it once you find its location?" Charley is not about to let Lou off the hook until he gets the whole picture.

"Once we know where the center is, we will do a coordinate transformation to adjust the data as if the observations had been made from that center. Does this seem reasonable, Charley?"

"You guys have been very thorough in developing your approach and the subject matter is certainly interesting. If I may, I'd like to make a suggestion that could possibly improve on the accuracy of your results."

"Go ahead, Charley, we can use any help you can give us."

"You mentioned how you plan to use star observations on record in the NASA archives. I'd like to suggest that we partner with NASA and access the Jemison Telescope to update our data base to the present time frame."

"That's an excellent idea, but it would mean a delay in the program to gather the number of points to calculate from. I'm talking of a data base in the neighborhood of two to three hundred sightings. These would be evenly distributed in sidereal coordinates each with its own latitude and longitude.

"As far as range goes, I would like sightings from close up, like Alpha Centauri, to – maybe a thousand light years away. Then our measurements should standardize on the most prominent hydrogen red emission line and its incremental shift to a longer wavelength."

"It should not be a problem, Lou. That instrument has been advertised as capable of doing all that you mentioned – and then some. I think it's certainly worth looking into."

"Accumulating this much information...the telescope is probably on its own mission. Do you think it could be done in a relatively short time, Charley?"

"I would venture a guess that in a couple of months it could produce all the data you'll be needing. Look – why don't I contact NASA to find out when the Jemison device is available? Meanwhile you can lay out a plan of your requirements as to number, range, and distribution of sightings.

"I'm sure this effort would be given a high priority on their list of experiments so you won't lose much time."

"If it's as easy as you make it sound, Charley, then it's worth the wait. In the meantime our software development group can put the final touches on the data processing algorithm to set it up for iterative calculations.

"I'm keeping my fingers crossed that these iterations trying out different universal mass values will converge to a best value. Otherwise the whole program may tank."

"There's the reason why you should go with your best shot, Lou. At least the Jemison telescope will give us observations that are close together in time. And then we should get the benefit of being away from atmospheric distortion – don't you agree?"

"Yes, absolutely," Louis answered. After months of intensive effort, it looked like he and his team of scientists would have a short breathing spell while awaiting the Jemison data. Who wouldn't agree to that?

In the meantime, the problems confronting the rest of the world showed no signs of abating.

Ever since Ben Davidson's vivid demonstration of the plight of the White race at the review seminar several months ago, the White population in predominantly White countries had shown a continuing downward trend. It was estimated that the world's White population had dropped three and one half percent since the White race went into suspended animation about fourteen months ago.

Time was working against humankind as Nature slowly sealed the fate of the White race. However, all was not lost. Those few fertile white enigmas continued to reproduce. Mary Davidson gave birth to her first son on January 17th – Jared Elbert Davidson weighed in at eight pounds five ounces.

27

FEBRUARY

Three months of waiting passed while the Jemison telescope gathered star fixes on 172 individual stars evenly distributed in the heavens. They ranged in distance from Earth, starting at twenty light years away to as far as three thousand light years. It was February 25th, when Louis Keck and his project team finally got a listing of the data by sidereal coordinates, date of sighting, time of day of sighting, distance from Earth, and the Doppler shift towards the red of the hydrogen emission line for each one of the sightings.

The data was in raw form and needed to be corrected for the fact that the Jemison telescope itself was not a stationary platform during the sightings. There were two such corrections to be made. First, the telescope was in orbit in an equatorial plane around the Earth making a complete revolution every 90 minutes at an altitude of 187 miles. That translated into a speed in orbit of 17,362 miles per hour, tangentially. Next, the Earth was orbiting the Sun once every 365 days at a distance of 93,000,000 miles. This translated into a tangential speed of 66,671 miles per hour as it revolved around the Sun.

Knowing the time of each sighting, located the Jemison in its two effective orbits relative to the coordinates of each star sighting. It was then a simple matter by trigonometric means to correct the data by removing the two velocity components. The end result was the receding velocity which had been calculated from the Red Shift for that star.

Correction for the star itself having a speed component in a galactic orbit was assumed to be negligible because of the much greater distance from the star to the center of mass to its galaxy. Observations of the stars in the past revealed practically no relative motion between star systems, which supported that assumption.

Once the data had been corrected for known errors, the task was to locate the center of the universe by using the nonlinear character of the Red Shift as a function of the distance from where the Big Bang took place. Efforts proceeded smoothly, using the computer program developed for that purpose, and the end result identified a location just outside of the Milky Way.

Next came the task of transforming coordinates on the data to relocate the vantage point to the center of the universe. A program was executed for each of the 172 star sightings using successive velocity away from the center of the universe, then serious number crunching got underway. The premise that the universe would someday stop expanding and then start to collapse back towards the center also assumed that all parts would reach their zenith at exactly the same time.

Louis Keck's approach to calculating the time to the Big Bang was to use each star sighting to produce its own equation of motion. If each equation was solved for time since the Big Bang, then the equations would become equal to each other at the moment expansion stopped. The problem was one of fitting the observed data in each case by trial and error, using a different total mass influencing the farthest star sighting. Each sighting at a lesser distance used an assigned percentage of that total mass as its gravitational mass.

The least square deviation was a technique to arrive at the best curve when interpreting empirical data. The best fit would occur for all 172 equations when the trial mass produced the minimum least squares deviation.

"The moment of truth has arrived," Lou said to his team. "I know we're anxious to test our hypothesis, so let it rip!"

The program they developed used an iterative scheme which automatically searched for the right mass by testing different values for the best fit. Hopefully, after a number of iterations, each succeeding trial mass would lead to a better result until small changes no longer yielded any improvement.

Pleased expressions appear on the faces of the team members observing the computer program in action. It was obvious that the computer iterations were gradually honing in on the most probable mass for the universe based on the best agreement in the 172 separate solutions.

The iterations continued automatically as the incremental change in the test mass decreased each time there was an overshoot in results. The process continued until the mass of the universe to the farthest star sighting was resolved to one part in about 70 billion.

The equations of motion for 172 separate star sightings plus one more for Earth's distance from the center of the universe were calculated.

The calculations for the time when the universe's expansion would come to a stop were executed. The answer came out – 18,347 billion years plus or minus 17.8 million years.

The calculation for the present age of the universe was then made. The answer revealed was the same – 18,347 billion years plus or minus 17.8 million years.

There was reason for a certain amount of elation over the results, for coming close to previous estimates of the age of the universe, but the feelings were accompanied by a good deal of disappointment.

"If nothing else is aided by our efforts, at least we have shown that the age of the universe can be calculated using what may be a novel technique," Lou remarked to his staff in an effort to cheer them up.

"The age calculation stacks up pretty well with prior ones – but the first result may be a puzzler.

"Maybe we've stumbled onto something connected with the times, especially with the strange events taking place around the world. In any case, this is no time to stop. Before we give up the whole idea as a futile effort, let's try a little optimization by fine-tuning some of our system constants – I mean the ones other than mass itself.

"OK? Let's give it one more try."

When the meeting broke up, Lou headed to his office. He, too, was feeling quite dejected over the mediocre results after such an intensive effort, but he hadn't wanted his dedicated team to sense it during their meeting.

"Hey, Lou, wait up!" Charley called as he caught up to Lou. "Why the somber mood? Like you told your team, this is no time to call it quits."

"I know, Charley. It's just that our expectations were so great and we fell so far short of the mark."

"Don't forget this was the first run of your computer program – and the results were not all that bad. You've heard the old – garbage in garbage out – saying about data processing. Well – you people have done a whole lot better on your first try.

"Like you said at the meeting – this is a time to do some fine tuning on your system constants. You might want to adjust the mass percent factor for each equation and make it more a function of the initial impulse during the Big Bang. Remember how the original impulse had a tail on it in your model?

"Then consider tossing out some of those data points that seem to contribute the most scatter in the results. I suspect that the most remote star sightings are not the most accurate, especially in the distance estimate."

"I haven't thrown in the towel yet, Charley. We still have a lot of work ahead of us."

The next four weeks were a busy period of rerunning programs several times where small changes were made in critical parameters to see if scatter in the results could be reduced significantly. Solutions were calculated for a wide range of combinations made up of small variations in parameters.

The corresponding effects on the calculations of age and time of the universe's expansion showed small swings in their magnitudes and the root mean square deviation or scatter, but they always came out equal to each other. The best combination yielded a value for age and time of expansion at 17.946 billion years plus or minus 6.4 million years.

Lou was completely preoccupied with the disappointing results produced so far. He spent more and more time at his office, exhausting every possibility he can think of to come up with more meaningful results.

On a particular night, already past eleven o'clock, Lou reviewed the results in hand, looking for a clue that might open up a new approach. Katy dropped in for a surprise visit.

"Hi, stranger. Haven't seen you for a while. Are you trying to avoid me?"

"You know me better than that, Hon. I'm getting no place with this project and I'm running out of ideas."

"For starters, Dear, it's time for a break. I know you haven't eaten, so I packed us a dinner, and we can eat right here in your office." She placed containers of food and silverware on a clear patch of desk.

"Frankly I'm a bit worried. It's not good for an old timer like you to work such long hours. Come now, set aside your paperwork, and let's get some nourishment in you. I brought us each a cup of hot vegetable soup and your favorite chicken sandwich. Your brain cells need it."

No question Lou was hungry. He had not eaten anything since lunch with Charley at the school cafeteria.

"Honey, this is delicious. Thank you for being a peach," Lou said, relishing his wife's preparations.

"Coffee?" Katy offered, opening up a thermos.

Lou smiled. He leaned back in his chair with his feet on his desk to slowly sip his coffee while Katy tidied up.

"I guess it won't be long before I have to bite the bullet and admit this whole project was for naught," Lou said. It's sure to be a big disappointment for the guys and gals who worked on the project with me."

"Now listen to me, Dear. I've known you for a good many years, and I've seen you survive through success and failure time and again. That's what research is about. You've told me many times that you learn from failures – isn't that true?"

"You know, Hon, it's refreshing just to sit here and have my words come back to haunt me," Lou teased. "Yes, life goes on in spite of our disappointments – only this time there's so much at stake. All these crazy results we've gotten seem to be telling us something. Why should the age of the universe and the time when it stops expanding come out to be the same?"

"You know something, Dear, I always wondered why you scientists are not very specific when you talk large numbers. It seems like something is either one million or two million but never anything in between. You've been telling me the past month about the age of the universe being 18 billion years. For all the sophisticated techniques that you have at your disposal, can't you work that out to a more exact figure?"

Lou couldn't believe what he was hearing. Katy had put her finger on what he and his colleagues had never even considered. The large uncertainty of 6 or 7 million years in their answers totally overshadowed the high resolution available to them if they reached out to the latest software developers to refine their program.

"Who told you to come here tonight, anyway? You've upset my whole train of thought. We'd better call it quits for today and head home," Lou said, pretending to be serious, but the look on his face was a dead giveaway.

"You just got a brainstorm didn't you? I can tell when your right ear twitches." Katy responded in her usual quick-witted fashion, and they both had a good laugh.

On the way home, Lou said, "Katy, I'm going to find out just how equal those two numbers really are."

Late the following afternoon, Lou had called a meeting to inform his team members that they'd partnered with Maxton Labs., the hottest tech firm in Silicon Valley and were going to redo calculations using a new program, tested and debugged, about to be released to the market. He introduced Shaila Chawla, Maxton's representative.

"Good morning, Ladies and Gentlemen, instead of rounding off and truncating numbers at intermediate steps during calculations, resolution will be preserved in every step of the program. Final answers produced will be rounded off to tenths of years. I'll upload your data this evening and in about 24 to 48 hours, I'll have results for you, which I'll share in a PowerPoint presentation."

Shaila was true to her word, and the team was reassembled two mornings later. The format on the screen was arranged in four columns per line with the following headings:

AGE OF UNIVERSE	EXPANSION TIME	DIFFERENCE	UNCERTAINTY

There were 34 sets of calculations on 34 lines of print. The first two entries on each line were 12 digit numbers representing years resolved down to tenths of years; the fourth entry was the uncertainty of those two numbers, also resolved to tenths of years.

The two large numbers per line covered a range of years from 18 billion down to 16 billion and the number pairs appeared to be very nearly the same.

The fourth column showed an uncertainty ranging between 6 and 18 million years.

The third column at first appeared to be a printing error hung up at +1.9 years on all 34 lines of print.

A closer inspection of the AGE OF UNIVERSE AND EXPANSION TIME entries on each line did show that they were indeed 1.9 years different with AGE the larger of the two.

"The hang up with these results is that we are coming up with a constant small difference between two large numbers when the uncertainty in either one of these numbers far exceeds that small difference," said Charley Stafford. "Is it possible that it has to do with the method used to calculate those numbers?" he asked Shaila.

Everyone was similarly dumbfounded with the unexpected.

"This data is correct – it's been run several times," Shaila said.

Herb Wilson from in-house computing operations had a couple of his own questions. "Would the fact that both numbers are calculated from similar equations explain what you are alluding to, Charley? If the two numbers are close in magnitude, isn't it conceivable they might be in error by exactly the same amount, but their difference would be unaffected, and therefore – may be accurate?"

At that point, Louis Keck could not wait to add his own comment. "In every one of our calculations we came up with a slightly different age, but let's not forget that in every case we calculated the span of time from the Big Bang to – TODAY."

"What you are telling us, Lou, is that the universe stopped expanding 1.9 years ago. Am I understanding you correctly?" Herb asked.

"That could well be, Herb. Put more precisely, it would have to be 1.9 years before the Jemison telescope made the measurements for us during that three-month period starting in December of last year.

"My concern is this: Can we make this kind of a claim based on the star sighting data that we used? The scientific community might frown upon our results and even figure this to be a hoax. We might be in for a lot of ridicule."

"It boils down to a matter of how to interpret our results," Charley was quick to add. "This situation is somewhat similar to the measurement of temperature which we did for a long period of time without knowing precisely where absolute zero was. We have made very accurate measurements of temperature differences in processes where our knowledge of absolute values was of no concern because we used reference points along the way such as the ice point for water, and so on."

"Charley, what you're saying is that our time reference in this case is today's time," Lou cut in. "But the absolute value of today's time doesn't matter. The important piece of information is the time the universe stopped expanding relative to today's time. We may have stumbled onto a viable technique for calculating that time interval only because the two absolute values are so close together and subject to exactly the same errors.

"I have no problem with that, Lou," Charley said. "As a matter of fact, I'm willing to go on record right now with the following claim:

THE EXPANSION OF THE UNIVERSE
CAME TO A STOP DURING LAST JANUARY!!!"

"That correlates with the time when the White race underwent some very weird experiences," Herb Wilson said, agreeing with Charley's statement.

"I don't think we want to go public with this possible discovery unless we get more positive results to confirm it," Lou said, weighing in. "Do you agree, Charley? It's much too skimpy as it stands to make such a claim."

"I agree with you 100 percent. It's possibly a major discovery of our times, and it's likely too much for mankind to handle right now. Any suggestions as to what we should do as a follow up?"

"How about we repeat the tests using the same star sightings with the Jemison telescope and repeat our calculations using the same algorithms as before, but change the time of the experiment," said Lou.

"My thoughts exactly. Let's proceed posthaste. I'll make arrangements with NASA to use the Jemison ASAP." Charley said, anxious to get started."Shaila, I'm assuming Maxton Labs would be available again to crunch the data for us, am I right?"

"Definitely. We're fully on board. And before you ask, confidentiality is guaranteed. It's understood how sensitive this could be."

Two months later the data from the Jemison telescope arrived and computations were run. Shaila presented the results. This time the difference between the age of the universe and the time it stopped expanding was a constant for all sightings at 2.6 years. The audience, mainly project personnel, went wild with the results.

"This is too much for us to break to the public," Charley excitedly announced. "I'll schedule a presentation to the Seminar Review Committee right away. In the meantime, let me say that all of you in this lab deserve a well-earned breathing spell after such an intensive effort. Let me be the first to congratulate you for a job well done; and this goes especially to you, Lou, for your outstanding program leadership."

Although Louis Keck's discovery of Nature's turnabout could help explain major changes taking place in the world, it didn't offer a solution to the desperate plight of the White race on Earth.

As of August 22nd, according to Ben Davidson's ongoing CENSUS program, the world's White population was estimated to have decreased almost seven percent since the birth rate went into limbo in October, two years prior.

The only encouraging newsmakers were those few fertile White anomalies. Mary Davidson, pregnant once again, was expecting her third child in early March.

28

SEPTEMBER

The Southwestern Institute of Technology in Austin, Texas, was the host location for the next program review seminar on September 17th.

It had become customary for Bob Armstrong, chosen as permanent chairman of the review committee at their first organizational meeting, to set the tone of each session with a few opening remarks before introducing the main speaker.

"Ladies and Gentlemen, the topic of discussion for our get together today represents another departure from most of the previous seminars which have been in specialized fields of medicine.

"You'll recall Ben Davidson's presentation on demographic studies a few months back. Ben certainly has provided us with a continuous population monitor during these critical times.

"Today's speaker is another representative from the physical sciences. His team of scientists have been studying the Big Bang theory in an effort to learn something about our origins. Some of the credit for including this activity in our overall research program must go to Dr. Charles Stafford who is also with us today. He had the foresight back when we first organized as an emergency research group in February of last year to recommend probing into the moment of creation itself.

"Our speaker is a bit older than most of us here today. He is the type of person who cannot stand the idleness of retirement after a very productive career in industry. So he chose to get back into research, but this time around he picked an academic environment which is why we are fortunate to have him with us on this occasion. Charley Stafford has a keen eye for selecting talent to work on his fusion research program here at the Institute.

"I take great pleasure in presenting Louis Keck, controls expert and theoretician."

After a solid round of applause, Lou has the floor to begin his presentation which is sure to raise some eyebrows among the prestigious members of the audience.

"First of all I would like to express my thanks to Dr. Armstrong for his very generous comments, to Dr. Stafford for taking me on as a member of his research team, and to all of you for showing such enthusiasm about the subject of my talk.

"My style is not one to keep you in suspense, so I will get right to the point. My colleagues and I have reason to believe that the universe reached the apex of its expansion phase three years ago, during the month of January. It has now begun a gravitational collapse back onto itself."

Everyone in the audience was caught off guard by such a totally unexpected revelation. The reaction covered the gamut from one of just plain awe, to disbelief, to skepticism, to utter amazement that anyone should have the nerve to suggest such a hoax.

For several minutes, Lou's presentation was interrupted by people in the audience muttering in a constant chatter their surprised reactions to each other.

"Please, let's get this meeting under control!" Bob Armstrong boomed out. "Give Lou a chance to explain how they came across this important discovery!!" The room quieted down.

"We are just as shocked as you are," Lou continued. "That's why we have not dared make a public announcement before this meeting. You are the first to know outside of the members of the project team and the data analysts."

He looked around the room as if pleading for a chance to tell them how they happened to stumble upon their findings.

For the next hour Louis Keck had the undivided attention of the audience as he described their project and how it evolved every step of the way to the final result. He went on to explain that the calculation of the difference between the expansion time and the present age of the universe was made possible only because the two events happened to have occurred at very nearly the same time.

At the end of his talk, he has left no doubt about the logic behind their conclusion. Furthermore, the time coincidence of all the other events that have taken place in the world, along with his latest claim, left no other choice but to at least consider the possibility of it being fact. There appeared to be general agreement among members of the audience that the universe could well be entering a contraction phase.

"The ramifications of this discovery could have far reaching consequences," Charlie Stafford commented from the audience. "We may be experiencing the end of a phase in nature and entering another which could be full of surprises. The events of the past two and a half years certainly bear this out."

There's not one smiling face in the entire room as the realization sank in that humankind may simply be a pawn, hardly visible in an arena so vast as the universe where immense processes were unfolding. Life as they knew it could be a tiny flicker of light about to be snuffed out in a universe that has veered in a new direction.

After serious discussion about how the predicament of the White race might fit in to this much bigger picture of what is happening in the universe, the conclusion was reached that present research in all areas of science must go on. As a last resort, the scientific community should at least try to develop an understanding of what was happening, even though it may not be able to exert control on the behavior of Nature's forces.

Scientific information *was* accruing. Great progress in the area of diagnostics has been made. Humanity was able to track its own gradual demise, which hopefully could be turned around if a medical breakthrough could be realized.

Man's last hope was probably in the field of genetics where activity was taking place at a feverish pace in a last desperation effort.

"To conclude," Bob Armstrong started, "I will remind you, that as scientists, we still have a major obligation to fulfill. The world populace must be told of this recent discovery and the uncertain future that looms ahead. Life is as mysterious as ever – we know that scientific processes, such as evolution, take billions of years to unfold, yet we are experiencing ramifications of significant magnitude in a blink. This is sure to foster intense unease among the inhabitants of our planet. Hopefully, continuing investigation will quell some of this fear of the unknown.

"The first person we will share this information with is the President of the United States. We will present a unified scientific front. The government should handle it from there."

Two days later a special meeting of the UN General Assembly in New York was televised worldwide, informing people on the planet that the forces of Nature had taken a new turn.

The news release was a carefully worded statement intended to avert a panic reaction that could become catastrophic. It emphasized that the universe had spent about 18 billion years expanding to its present size and was expected to undergo a contraction of a similar time duration. During this second phase, life as they knew it would gradually be phased out. People were cautioned not to despair because the time scales employed by Nature in executing its evolutionary processes were so long that it would be thousands of generations before people living on Earth would have to seek an alternate universe to reside in.

Even after reassurances that life should continue on a normal path, the inability of the White race to procreate remained too big a problem for humanity to accept as just another of Nature's unpredictable actions. The persistent question that no one seemed able to answer was: Why should the White race be singled out as the first human species to depart this planet?

જી

Meanwhile, Tom and Molly Curtis relocated to the San Diego area so Tom could more actively participate in his critical program at the National Laboratory for Genetics. He had been on a sabbatical from Kennebec College for an indefinite period since the move to the West coast back in early September. Research programs like the one he was engaged in could sometimes take years before results – good or bad – were realized. He and Molly rented a condominium in a quiet section of La Jolla overlooking the coast with miles of gorgeous beaches which Molly had taken full advantage of. She was completely recovered from her serious illness. Although she had gone through breast reconstruction, she felt a tank suit was fine for swimming, and she'd leave the bikinis to the teenagers.

"Isn't the Southern California climate so fantastic this time of the year, Dear?" Molly had remarked to Tom after they had settled into their new living quarters back a year and a half ago. "I think we'll enjoy our stay here very much, don't you? There's so much we can do on weekends, visiting places we've never seen, even besides taking advantage of the beach which is so handy."

"I'm sorry to disappoint you, Moll, but I suspect you won't be seeing much of me for the duration of this research program," Tom had replied. We have a kickoff meeting tomorrow morning and all hell is going to break loose after that. I don't expect much leisure time visiting and relaxing on the beaches."

Of course Tom's predication had been right. He'd had no more than three or four days off since the start of the program. But Molly was an independent soul and practically became a native Californian. Her healthy looking tan contrasted sharply with Tom's laboratory pallor.

Who would have thought three year ago that Molly would once again become a picture of health as if never stricken by cancer. What strange ways Nature had of demonstrating its authority. Molly felt grateful to not have become a burden on Tom during such a critical time.

Aside from two trips Molly had taken to visit family back East, and Tom's travels to attend review seminar meetings once a month at various locations all over the country, Europe, and once in Japan, the two had stayed put in San Diego.

So far, attempts to characterize human genes as to racial properties had not been successful. Even with the most sophisticated laboratory equipment, Tom and his team of experts had not been able to break the genetic code as it might relate to race. The complex DNA molecule, the fundamental building block of the human reproductive system, was like an encyclopedia of detail describing each human as a unique living organism. The double helical structure of the molecule replicated itself over and over again during the growth process, repeating exactly the physical traits and properties that made an individual a unique life form.

Even when two persons mated and conception took place, the DNA structure of the embryo was unique in that it was composed of a combination of traits inherited from the DNA of each parent.

Tom and his colleagues were coming around to the notion that the uniqueness of each DNA, regardless of race, completely overshadowed any property in its structure that might signify a racial trait.

In spite of the setbacks they had experienced in their research, Tom felt the missing clue that could provide an answer, and hopefully a means of correcting the dilemma of the White race, was awaiting discovery. His in-vitro fertilization experiment back at Kennebec College almost two years ago provided motivation to continue his search for answers.

During this same trying period, Ben Davidson had been totally engrossed in two activities which took up all of his time. His demographic program at NASA required refinements in the computer software. This kind of activity in computer science was commonplace as never-ending improvements always strived for the ideal program.

Nevertheless, the global infrared population monitor had been fully operational for quite some time. The information it had provided was certainly not encouraging, but at least it kept track of the slow decline in population throughout the Western world.

Ben's other activity had been on the home front where he and Mary were busy bringing up a family. Mary had given birth to Benjamin Louis Davidson, Jr. on March 11th. He weighed in at eight pounds six ounces. Since Krissy's birth almost three years ago, the Davidsons had averaged one new addition per year. Needless to say, Ben and Mary had their hands full with three young infants needing constant attention.

"We sure have been making up for lost time, haven't we? All those years purposely not getting you in the family way because of my failing heart, and look at us today," Ben teased Mary as they finished bathing the children and put them to bed. Little Ben was three months old and sweet boy that he was, had begun sleeping through the night.

"Yes, we sure have, Honey. That heart donor from New England must have been some bedroom cowboy. How else can you explain it?"

"Seriously though, don't you think we've been unbelievably fortunate during our years together? First, my career went exactly as we hoped it would at the Space Center. Then when I got sick, Dr. Armstrong came to the rescue with a replacement heart. And now we have three wonderful children, even though we had a late start. Don't you often wonder how this is possible in the midst of the turbulent times the world is experiencing?"

"I don't have to be a scientist to agree with what you are saying, Hon. I just hope whoever is up there pulling the strings also has our wellbeing included in his plans. When I think of the uncertain future of our kids, I'm terribly worried about what's in store for them." Tears came into Mary's eyes as she looked to Ben for some assurance that their safety would be taken care of.

Ben took Mary in his arms to hug and comfort her; she was an especially loving person where her family was concerned.

"You shouldn't worry so much, Dear. We have to live our lives one day at a time. We cannot dwell on what may happen to us in the immediate future based on long term changes taking place in the universe. Civilization has been around a very short time in terms of the age of that universe, and it is sure to be here, by our measure of time, for a good long while to come."

"What about the decreasing White population that you and the people at the Space Center are keeping track of every day?"

"No one is coming up with answers on that problem."

"Then why are you and I able to have children?" Mary asked.

"Some of the best minds in the world are working on that problem and we must have faith they will come up with answers. Don't forget that most of the people in the world are still producing – along with you and me. It's a matter of finding out what's so different about the rest of the White race, and then reactivating its productive capability."

"Don't get any ideas about increasing our own family size, honey child. I'm not pregnant and don't plan to be — we have reached our quota," said Mary, regaining her composure.

"Actually," Ben said, "there were rumblings at the last review seminar, about testing people such as ourselves. I think they might have started down that route. Because you've been pregnant, more than not over these past few years, I don't think they wanted to put us on the list yet. But would you be open to that now?" Ben asked.

"What would that entail; do you know?" Mary asked.

"It's in preliminary stages, but probably tissue samples, I imagine."

"How could we say no, when we have been blessed with three children and the vast majority of other White couples can't conceive? Of course we have to help," Mary said.

"Okay, I'll let Tom Curtis know that we're ready," Ben said.

❧

The rest of the world populace did not take its questionable destiny lightly. The average person was at a loss to interpret the latest news releases about the state of the universe.

The prophets of doom were demoralizing a large segment of the population with warnings that the end of the world was close at hand. A large number of people believed that their only recourse was to prepare to meet their maker. Church attendance rose a thousandfold in every religious denomination.

As always, the profiteers lurked in the background waiting for the right moment to make their sales pitch to the vulnerably desperate. They assured safe passage to the hereafter – for the right price.

Others became panic-stricken, barely able to function and eventually totally despondent. Unfortunately, a good number of these people committed suicide rather than face a more terrible fate.

Another large segment of the population held on to their sanity and were determined to cope with world changes in the best way possible. They placed their hopes on the scientific community to come up with suitable solutions.

Nature had revealed the extent of its power and humanity its powerlessness to fight the course of emerging events. Natural history would prove the greatest teacher for showing how major calamities of the past were dealt with. The answer had always been to adapt; the solutions forthcoming from the scientific community would hopefully reflect this timeless wisdom of acceptance.

29

Ever since Louis Keck's seminar presentation announcing the end of the universe's expansion phase, the program review meetings had become more frequent. The problems facing humanity had taken on a far greater dimension. Meeting agendas included a wide variety of subjects going back to creation itself. Participants at the seminars included philosophers and theologians, in addition to the medical experts, the related sciences and the physical sciences that had dominated meeting agendas up to now.

What connection did the White race being in limbo have with the universe starting to shrink? The philosophers in the group liked to expound on the expansion phase of the universe as being a period of creation, and conversely, the contracting universe as the undoing of creation.

It was logical to assume that creation was not a period of chaos, but rather a sequential process, where each completed step became a building block for the next step.

Immediately following the Big Bang when matter was heaved outward in space in all directions, future stars gathered in some of this stray matter to become localized centers of mass. When these centers of mass had accumulated enough of this matter through gravity, they ignited from their own compressive forces to become stars, although with an accompanying release of energy, which was much smaller than the Big

Bang. In fact, most stars didn't have the explosive power to blow themselves completely apart and yet they continued burning from their own gravitational compression.

When the stars were born, they in turn ejected large chunks of matter, which in some cases became planets which became trapped in orbits around these stars. Other chunks of matter that were remnants from the Big Bang were captured by these same stars to also become planets. Our own solar system had planets that may have originated from one or the other of these two sources.

The stars themselves, in addition to being constantly attracted by gravity back to where they came from at the center of the universe, were subject to other forces coming from centers of galaxies. They were actually in their own orbit around the centers of mass of these galaxies, much like planets orbiting a sun.

The philosophers argued that processes took place in their proper sequential time setting to become the expanding universe familiar to us. The birthing of stars within the universe never ceased, as centers of mass continued collecting stray mater from the void of space.

All of these events have been taking place as a function of time – since the beginning of time. It had been a perpetual explosion that we as observers view as a one-time snapshot in our time. Although part of that evolutionary process, our turn in the sequence of creation took place in relatively recent times.

Now that the universe had exhausted its outward momentum, it logically followed that the next phase would be to collapse in on itself. It was reasonable to assume that the universe would undergo its own un-creation. The phenomenon was a highly unique experience to all of its constituent parts and could the effects on biological life on Earth be other than shattering?

The theoretical physicists advanced their concept of reversibility; how in such a system, the last in – first out rule applies. If the undoing of creation was to take place, it would follow that the last product of the creation would be the first to exit the scene. The suggestion of reversibility cast a negative prediction on events happening on Earth. Was the White race the last product of creation? Why were other races still thriving and their numbers increasing? The information that had surfaced in recent years seemed to confirm what the theoreticians alluded to: the White race could well be doomed to extinction in the foreseeable future.

The medical experts had their own explanations for what was taking place in the world: a genetic anomaly. Genetically related diseases among Whites seemed to have become a thing of the past. Then the reproduction capability of the White race shut off. There could only be one answer – White humans' biological clocks may have come to a standstill.

The genetic code, unique for each living being on Earth, must share something in common that allowed members of a species to reproduce. Conversely, any deviation of that genetic code from what was considered normal for that species, resulted in an abnormality in the cell structure, which had been the source of many incurable illnesses.

It appeared that there was a built-in racial factor residing within man's genetic makeup. It benefited the White race through resistance to deadly diseases, yet prevented reproduction.

Finally, members of the clergy and theologians had their say about the predicament facing mankind. They referred to the book of Genesis as the step-by-step record of the Creation. The events that had taken place since the Big Bang could be accounted for in the writings about Genesis. The seven days it took the Creator to complete the project brought us right up to the present time. The historians who recorded their revelations of these events used the measure of time most familiar to them. Little did they realize that the process had taken some seventeen or so *billion* years.

The ultimate product of the Creation was humanity itself. Different from other living species, it was endowed with a greater amount of intelligence by the Creator to see how man would fare among them. Where most creatures managed to survive by instinct, humans had the additional capability to reason, which should give them a considerable edge in the struggle for survival.

During man's relatively short tenure of a million or so years on the planet, man had made ample use of natural resources available to improve his lifestyle. It could be said that he had made great strides in developing civilized society. However, man's superior intellect and free will allowed undesirable traits to surface.

The Ten Commandments described in the Old Testament were intended to be a code of behavior for the human race, but they had all been violated by man, time and time again, through the ages, to suit his own purposes. Could it be that the wrath of God had finally been aroused? Had man gone a step too far in squandering the Earth's natural resources to satisfy his own selfish motives? What about racial prejudice that was too often the cause of major conflicts in the world throughout the history of mankind? Had man sunk to a level of decadence during his tenure on the planet such that he had lost faith in the Supreme Being who had made his very existence possible?

Perhaps humankind had reached its day of reckoning with the Creator, and it would have to account for its destructive past actions. The White race might just be the first to be made to pay for its sins.

The review seminars went on with dissertations on every conceivable subject – each trying to rationalize what was taking place in the world today. The conclusions in every case were the same – the White race, and most likely the rest of mankind, has begun its departure from the planet Earth.

As time went on, all that the experts had reported was generally accepted as true and non-conflicting. The mood of the world's White populace became one of despair as the realization sank in that their tenure on Earth had entered its terminal phase.

Bob Armstrong couldn't bring himself to accept theories suggested at these meetings without questions of his own. During his concluding remarks after the latest seminar presentation, he aired his reservations about the somber mood that had set in.

"Ladies and Gentlemen, the past two plus years has been a period of scientific enlightenment, but we seem to be coming up with rationalizations that accept a forecasted doomsday.

"Certainly, we can't just give up – there is too much at stake. These seminars have served a good purpose, and there is no question in my mind that they should continue. However, don't you agree that our focus needs to be on possible solutions to get us out of this mess?"

"What more can we do at this stage?" came a question from the audience.

"We have exhausted about every scientific avenue available to us, and everyone is leading to the same conclusion," called out another voice.

"If you have a new approach in mind, why don't you let us in on it?" said someone.

"I can appreciate what you are saying, and I wouldn't doubt for a minute that the participants in our seminars have done excellent research in their areas of expertise. All I am suggesting is that we take an objective look at our results one more time on the chance that we overlooked something important.

"Many of us in this room have witnessed certain events during the past two or so years which have left an unforgettable impression on us. In my own medical specialty, which is as you know, organ transplant surgery, I've had the very satisfying experience of seeing most of my patients make a total recovery from major surgery with no sign whatsoever of organ rejection.

"Granted these miraculous recoveries have taken place since planetary changes began, but I am amazed at how some of these patients have fared since receiving their replacement organs. One of these individuals is with us here today. I'm sure you all remember Ben Davidson, who gave us an excellent and, as I recall, vivid presentation at the NASA labs in Houston on his demographic research."

Bob motioned to Ben to stand up to be recognized, and he received a round of applause.

"Now I would like to tell you a bit more about this individual – my good friend from NASA l," Bob continued. "Ben Davidson has been living with a donor heart since the aforementioned January. I performed the surgical procedure, and I have seen this man undergo phenomenal recovery without needing anti-rejection drugs during the entire period – right up to the present time.

"I certainly do not want to lay claim to an extraordinary operating technique after Louis Keck's revelation of the state of the universe. But…you know, let me digress for a moment." Bob paused. "The wife of another of our members, Dr. Tom Curtis, experienced a complete recovery from terminal cancer. Tom – please stand and be recognized. Molly's health went from dire to optimum during the same time period as Ben's."

Tom Curtis also got a round of applause as he acquiesced to Bob Armstrong's friendly recognition.

"Now – back to what I was saying. Ben Davidson not only has made a total recovery from heart surgery, but he and his wife, Mary, decided it was time to start a family, after postponements due to Ben's career obligations and the deteriorating heart condition that he had.   Well – within a span of the last three years, these two produced three healthy children – in spite of the present state of suspended animation being experienced by the White race. As I said earlier – this is no time to surrender to a hopeless fate, Ladies and Gentlemen."

"We have to concentrate on finding solutions to our problem – because there have been exceptions to our present dilemma and it is important that we find out why. Ben and Molly, along with other couples similarly blessed with progeny, are about to participate in a genetic study that could imminently alter the current status."

A rousing cheer went up in the auditorium and Tom couldn't help blushing scarlet from the attention.

"Please don't become disheartened; don't give up on your present research. We have come a long way in the last three years, and the answers we are looking for may be very close at hand. Thank you for being here today, and may our next seminar be as informative as our past ones."

Bob Armstrong's closing comments may have spurred on the team of researchers in their quest for answers, but the rest of the world…the populace despondently awaited its fate.

30

MARCH

One and a half years since his move to San Diego, Tom Curtis and his team of genetics experts, realized that DNA molecules regardless of which human individual they represented, were as much alike in structure as they were different.

The double helix, trademark of the DNA chain for every human being, contained a complete description of that individual for each physical characteristic, down to the minutest detail such as eye and hair color, bone structure, facial features, frame size, height, and hundreds of other peculiarities that made him or her unique. Similarly, the individual's mental acuity, learning capacity, and other singular neurological traits were also inscribed within that same molecule.

One could think of the DNA molecule as a detailed recipe for building a human being different from every other human being in the world. The concept not only held true for humans: every life form, whether animal or vegetable, also had its unique molecular structure.

Tom and his colleagues had probed the mysteries of DNA with the most modern of instruments ranging from electron microscopes, magnetic nuclear resonance analyzers, mass spectrographs, and a host of other sophisticated electronic hardware. They managed to unravel and expose the structure of the double helix. The bulk of the DNA molecule was comprised of atoms commonly found in organic molecules such as hydrocarbons. Hydrogen, oxygen, nitrogen, and carbon were the elements mostly in use, but there were also elements in the halide family such as chlorine, bromine, iodine, and fluorine to be found attached.

Trace amounts of many metallic elements such as boron, zinc, copper, calcium, iron, and others were also present.

The complexity of the molecule manifested itself in the cross-linkages that tied the elements together. Every linkage in the structure was part of the code representing an individual living being. Interestingly, DNA molecules from any one person were found to be identical. Similar molecules from several individuals may have looked similar, but upon scrutiny, the fine structure revealed numerous differences. Even the DNA of an offspring was found to be different from the DNA of either parent.

So far, the massive effort to identify a racial characteristic within the DNA molecular structure had proven futile. Every time a difference attributable to race was thought to have been discovered between DNAs taken from individuals of different races, the same difference ultimately showed up in DNAs taken from individuals of the same race.

Consequently, the hope of eventually doing gene splicing to modify a person's DNA in a favorable way to reactivate his or her ability to reproduce was at a standstill. The most recent effort had been to use the latest technique developed in the field of biotechnology for this purpose. It utilized a harmless form of bacteria as a viral carrier to implant the modified DNA into the recipients system where it could multiply and become integrated by the host system. Unfortunately, this led to one more dead end.

Tom felt constantly frustrated. He was in a quandary as to what to do next. The results from every conceivable test so far had not yielded the kind of information he was looking for. He felt totally exhausted from long hours spent at the labs with no letup, even on weekends.

Molly noticed her husband's haggard expression in recent weeks – almost as if he were a defeated man with no one to turn to for help. During one of his rare appearances for dinner, she knew she had to snap him out of his mood of desperation.

"Honey, you are going to take a week off from this crazy schedule you've been on for the last couple of years. You need a vacation of some kind to gain some distance from this genetics puzzle and shift your perspective. If you don't refresh your mind and spirit, how can you expect to maintain any kind of efficiency?"

"I hear what you're saying, Moll, but I don't know how to relax anymore. It seems like everything we've tried for the past two plus years has failed – and time is running out on all of us. You realize that, don't you? This whole project haunts me, and I don't know what else to do but keep trying – only we're running out of ideas.

"Maybe you are right. I should get away for a week and move beyond these disappointments. We're about to start working with the DNA of White couples who are conceiving, but unless we develop a fresh approach, it will be one more useless experiment."

"Tom, how about Lake Tahoe? It's ski season, and I know of a condo we can have for a week starting this Sunday. We can rent the gear we need once we get there. How about it? Do you think you would enjoy some time in the snow after all these years away from the slopes?"

"You're making me an offer I can't refuse – but Sunday is only three days from now. I'm not sure I should take time off on such a short notice. What would the rest of my team think if their leader took off suddenly, right before a major project?"

"Listen to me, Honey. You've had the least amount of time off of anyone on your project; you are long overdue for time to replenish yourself. The lab can run without you for a week. And, don't you think it's likely that if you return to work refreshed, it will boost their morale too?"

Tom knew he had to get away for a while. He felt grateful for Molly's gentle push to make it happen.

Molly took care of the preparations: firmed up the condo reservations, got airline tickets, arranged for a rental car, and bought the winter clothes they'd need. The week that followed was a real delight, but certainly not one of inactivity.

Tom and Molly enjoyed the ski slopes every day except for the one day they took a side trip to Carson City to visit the casinos. They would not soon forget it because Molly hit a jackpot on a dollar slot machine. The payoff was over seven hundred dollars. They dined at a different restaurant every night and went to a couple of nightclub shows during the week.

Most evenings were spent sitting in front of the fireplace, which they made ample use of, as a reminder of cold winter nights back in Maine. They chatted about the day's activities and enjoyed good laughs kidding each other about spills each had taken on downhill runs.

On their last night at Tahoe, Tom and Molly were talking about the good time they'd had and how they should do this more often.

"You know what, Molly? I almost dread going back to work. It seems like I'm still on square one after close to two years of wasted effort. The only tangible piece of information we have about the White race going sterile is that last experiment we did back at Kennebec before coming here. Remember the in-vitro fertilization tests we ran to confirm the loss of White man's ability to reproduce?"

"Yes, Hon – that's when I was your laboratory assistant. Before I became a woman of leisure with no responsibility except feeding you and getting you to work on time."

"Well, I don't take that for granted, that's for sure. Anyway, I've been thinking about what Bob Armstrong said at a recent seminar. We should be taking a second look at what's been done already on the chance that some significant finding was left incomplete."

"What could that be, Honey? You're such a thorough individual. I've never known anybody more meticulous than you are in your own area of expertise."

"Listen to this, Moll. The test matrix that I generated actually proved that the White race still has the ability to produce offspring. The problem is White people cannot mate successfully among themselves. The answers lie somewhere in the fertilization process. There has to be an inhibitor present which prevents White sperm from penetrating a White egg to achieve conception."

"So – what are you telling me? The problem has nothing to do with reproductive genes? Are you going to concentrate on a study of how conception actually takes place?"

Tom excitedly nodded. "I have state-of-the-art equipment at my disposal, much better than what was available at Kennebec College. We can design sophisticated experiments in fertilization. First of all – if there is a chemical inhibitor either in sperm or eggs or both, from members of the White race, we should be able to find it. I think a chemical analysis of both male sperm and female eggs is in order. Like in the previous fertilization tests we ran, we'll focus on specimens from three races – Black, Asian, and White."

Molly saw Tom's enthusiasm return; that's the nature of research. Scientists experienced many more disappointments than successes over the course of trying out new ideas or testing new theories. Tom was no exception, she reminded herself, but also felt proud that during his career he had experienced his share of triumphs.

Upon his return to San Diego, Tom Curtis met with members of his team to discuss the upcoming tests to be carried out at the genetics lab. His energized outlook was contagious. Test specimens of sperm and eggs would be obtained from healthy volunteer donors for extensive analysis using the laboratory's mass spectrograph. The donors would consist of a male and a female in each designated races. They'd establish a baseline of information. If differences in the chemical composition of the test specimens were in evidence, then further investigation would follow to determine the reason for those differences, and they'd be ready to move on to testing the White couples who were reproducing anomalies.

The tests were essentially repeats of prior tests on DNA molecules, only this time around, the specimens under study are the components from which life itself originated. It took about two weeks to select suitable volunteers and to wait for the opportune moment of ovulation, in the case of the female subjects, to obtain the necessary specimens.

The series of analyses using the mass spectrograph were uneventful as each specimen was analyzed and the results presented by a pen recorder in the form of a continuous graphical chart much like a histogram. The chart paper was pre-labeled by atomic weight and the corresponding chemical element by name, starting with hydrogen since it had the lowest atomic weight, and progressing in sequence to the heaviest – uranium – in the event of their detection in the sample under study. The entire record for each analysis was ten inches wide and ran to a total length of about five feet which covered hydrogen at an atomic weight of one mass unit at one end of the record to uranium at the opposite end at its maximum atomic weight of 239 mass units.

The final result for each of the test specimens would show a continuous pen recording where the presence of each element in the sample appeared as a pen deflection coinciding with the atomic weight for that element. The magnitude of the deflection was proportional to the amount of that element present in the sample specimen. The absence of an element in a test specimen was signified by a zero pen deflection at its assigned location in the output sequence.

On all six records, the distribution of chemical elements present encompassed all of the elements found in the prior DNA analyses. However, as might have been expected, there were additional elements present in the three sperm specimens, not present in the females' egg specimens, and vice versa.

The identical composition of the three specimens from each donor sex was somewhat of a disappointment to Tom. He had hoped to see differences that could give them a lead on identifying a White race inhibitor – but no such luck.

In any case, he planned to bring the records with him to the next seminar meeting in three days in Chicago. Even though the seminar topic scheduled for discussion was not in his present field of research, the current interest in genetics activity had been on an upswing, and there were bound to be questions concerning his experimental program. Besides, he had a few questions of his own, on subject matter lying outside his area of expertise.

The Chicago meeting like past meetings of the seminar group proved to be equally interesting. The guest speaker was from the Los Alamos Radiation Laboratory and he gave a dissertation on theoretical physics, which basically supported Louis Keck's prior talk on the Big Bang and creation.

At the conclusion of the meeting, Tom Curtis joined Bob Armstrong, Louis Keck, and Ben Davidson for lunch at McCormick Place on the lake front. The four men had become quite friendly on a professional level during the past two years and they often shared a meal together after meetings before returning home. Their wide-ranging areas of expertise could be counted on for interesting conversation.

Tom was quick to grab the opportunity to get some answers to his questions after the hostess sat them at their table. The mass spectrograph data in his briefcase had him a bit perplexed.

"Alright you guys. Who is the expert on mass spectrographs among you? I'd like to find out how these darn gadgets work because I have test data with me that has me buffaloed. Either my equipment isn't working properly or we may be on the verge of learning something about the White race's state of suspended animation."

The other three men were taken aback by such a profound statement, but they've grown accustomed to the element of surprise as a gimmick for getting attention. However, Tom was a respected scientist, not usually prone to such antics.

"What are you saying, Tom? Sounds to me like you're onto something big." Bob Armstrong was curious. "We'd better schedule you for another seminar one of these days. Are you about ready for one?"

"Not just yet, Bob. It depends upon what you guys can tell me about these chemical analysis records I brought. First of all – do you remember the report I gave in in-vitro fertilization some time back? Well – this latest experiment kind of picked up where that last one left off. After two or so years of DNA analysis trying to identify a racial factor in reproductive genes – and without success – I figured I had to try something drastically different, even if it did not seem logical.

"What I have done, Gentlemen, is to chemically analyze test specimens of sperm and eggs on a hunch – maybe we'd discover something significant. That's why I brought the results with me, because the spectrograph records show identical chemical contents from one record to another – except for a variation in the shape of the pen trace where the element, zinc, normally appears on the record. Would you like to see for yourselves what I'm talking about?"

Tom opened his briefcase and took out the six rolls of spectrograph records held together with rubber bands. He unraveled the first one to show a continuous pen recording with blips appearing where certain elements had been detected. The blips took on the shape of the element they represented based on the number of isotopes that made up that element.

"Bob, as a surgeon, it may be a while since you've had to think about this area of science, so would you like a refresher?" Tom asked.

"Much appreciated, thanks," Bob answered.

"Okay, isotopes in a particular element have the same chemical properties because they share in common the number of protons in their nucleus, but they have slightly different atomic masses because the number of neutrons also in their nucleus is different. Protons and neutrons have nearly the same mass and are described as having one unit of mass. Because the mass spectrograph performs its analysis based on the atomic mass of the elements, the isotopes are clearly evident in the process."

Louis Keck examined the record with great interest; he worked his way from the beginning where Hydrogen was indicated and progressed along the record to Carbon, then Nitrogen, Oxygen, and on to the heavier elements. When he got to Zinc, he saw only one blip, which indicated only one isotope for that element. He knew in an instant this wasn't normal because Zinc is known to be made up of five isotopes.

"You're right, Tom," Louis said. "Something is definitely awry in this record. Do all six records show the same distortion?"

Ben Davidson examined the other records trying to see what Lou was talking about.

"They all appear to have the same one blip characteristic where Zinc is supposed to be," Ben agreed.

"Look at all six records side by side," Tom said. "The male and female traces are a bit different from each other, but if you pair them up by race as I've noted on each one, what do you see as a difference between races?" Tom directed them to the Zinc element, which is what had him baffled.

"This is phenomenal, Tom. Is it possible you've discovered a racial factor? Each race has a different isotope of Zinc to identify it." Bob was obviously hopeful at this point, but suppressed his excitement, knowing there was a good possibility of an error.

"If there's a malfunction in the instrument causing this, it would have to be an extreme coincidence for the recordings to come out the way they have," Lou remarked with some confidence. "I've had experience with mass spectrographs."

"What about the previous analyses on DNA, Tom? Do they indicate a similar characteristic?" Ben asked.

"I happen to have brought some of those with me also. The presence of Zinc on those records is like we would normally expect. Here – see for yourselves. There are clearly five isotopes describing this element."

"Whoa baby, would you allow me to take a stab at summarizing your findings, Tom?" Bob Armstrong, a brilliant mind, synthesized information with impressive speed.

"Of course, you're the chairman," Tom joked.

"What you are showing us here today is positive evidence of a racial factor in the human reproductive process. Apparently this racial identifier is a transient phenomenon which only serves a function during the mating of two individuals. Otherwise, why wouldn't the same characteristic show up in the DNA molecule itself? Nonetheless, it's probably a good bet that this racial tag originates from the DNA code, and is included as part of the components of reproduction as they are produced in the body.

"Finally, there is still a chance that this is conjecture at this point in time. In fact, we don't yet know how this relates to the White race being in limbo. I gather you are not ready to go public with your findings until you've had time to recheck your results. Am I being too conservative, Tom, or possibly am I speaking out of turn?"

"No no! I agree with you one hundred percent, Bob. My only reason for bringing this up today was to use you as a sounding board to see if you would confirm my suspicion. Conclusions about the data would obviously be premature. The tests were run during this past month on a very small donor group. I would like to keep this information under wraps until we can obtain additional data from a larger test group."

"Good show, Tom. I still want to schedule you for a presentation on your findings whenever you feel ready," said Bob, beaming.

"Thank you, and Ben," Tom said, "looks like we'll need you and your wife's DNA pretty soon."

"Just say the word, Tom. It will be an honor to support your work – exciting stuff."

The following month was an extremely busy period for Tom Curtis and his team of researchers. Mass spectrograph data was obtained from a group of volunteers comprised of twenty male/female pairs from the Black, Asian, and White races. The results provided positive proof that a racial factor existed in sperm and eggs.

So far, only members of the three most populace world races had been tested, but there was good reason to test others. It would scientifically clarify if as theorized by the famous anthropologist, Margaret Mead, certain culturally indigenous races were "pure."

For the time being, the newly discovered Z-Factor provided a positive method of racial identification from the following Zinc isotopes:

Asian Race Designator	—	**Zn64**
Black Race Designator	—	**Zn66**
White Race Designator	—	**Zn68**

The isotopes were chemically the element Zinc, because they each had 30 protons in their nuclei. They had different atomic weights only because the number of neutrons in their respective nuclei ranged from 34 to 36 to 38. There still existed the possibility of two other races designated by the remaining Zinc isotopes at atomic weights 67 and 70.

It was believed that most elements present in the universe were created at the time of the Big Bang. The reaction was so violent and spontaneous that the present compositions of all elements were the stable remnant mass combinations that survived after the other unstable combinations disappeared through radioactive decay.

∽

Bob Armstrong had maintained close contact with Tom Curtis ever since their meeting in Chicago in April. He was anxious to schedule Tom for a presentation of his findings about the racial factor which could hold the key to the reactivation of the White race.

The date was June 24th, when Tom finally broke the news to the review committee about the Z-Factor being the part of the genetic code which identified the true race of a human being. The meeting was held at the National Genetics Laboratory in San Diego with about two hundred scientists in attendance.

The audience was truly in awe as he explained in great detail what had been accomplished during their research program. At the end of his talk, Tom emphasized that what had been done thus far was only a first step in their quest to reactivate the White race. There was no guarantee of success, but the discovery of the Z-Factor was certainly considered an essential and necessary step on the path to a solution.

"What makes you think that your Z-Factor has anything at all to do with the conception of children?" The question was asked from one of the skeptics in the audience.

"At this point in time, I have to be honest with you – we don't know for sure what the connection is. I will tell you this much, however. I'm sure that all of you present are aware, from the news media accounts, of the continuing growth in population among biracial groups. In fact, there has been a noticeable increase in racially mixed marriages during the past two years, most likely for the reason that White people are desperate to become parents and have dropped their prejudices – as both a way to enjoy the experience of family life and stave off the fear of extinction.

"In any case, our ongoing screening program is including volunteer subjects who are Whites married to Blacks; and Whites married to Asians. Interestingly, the adult offspring of these couples – who were also tested – are found to have dual race designators in their Z-Factor. It is too early to draw positive conclusions from this bit of information, but it does appear that the Z-Factor plays some kind of a role in the process of procreation.

"In closing, I would like to remind you that the White race is an endangered species on this planet. Our present task is of paramount importance, if we are to save it – hopefully without compromise. Thank you all for listening."

Tom Curtis and his research team made noteworthy progress, but the remaining task of turning the right key to restart White man's biological clock was yet to reveal itself.

While widespread publicity ensued and praise was liberally bestowed upon the team of scientists for a well-deserved accomplishment, the time to bear down for the ultimate solution was more urgent than ever. The entire world anxiously awaited news of a favorable breakthrough.

31

SEPTEMBER

The monumental task of finding the secret which made it possible for two individuals of the White race to mate and successfully produce offspring, was probably the most complex and least understood problem ever to face humankind.

Up until recently, the capability of living species on the planet to increase their numbers by procreation was taken for granted. It seemed that Nature intended for life forms of all kinds to flourish and experience unlimited improvements in quality via the breeding process. For Whites, that privilege had been rescinded.

Ever since the seminar meeting when he disclosed the existence of the Z-Factor, Tom Curtis and his team of scientists had been working 24/7 trying to discover how to override its effect as an inhibiting agent in the breeding of the White race.

Tom's brain was wholly engaged. *The prevention of conception based on the coincident presence the lone Zinc68 isotope in the male sperm and female egg is nothing short of a miracle. Why is this the only combination that didn't work?*

Furthermore, how is it possible for the human body to selectively separate out the single Zinc isotope that identifies its race? Isotope separation from our experiences during the World War II development of the Atom Bomb was a formidable task. Only one isotope of Uranium, U235, was known to be fissionable; and separating it from the other two isotopes of that element proved to be a very complex and difficult process. And now, science discovers that the human machine has been separating isotopes on a routine basis ever since the dawn of its existence?

The debate over the relationship between science and religion had long raged. Tom and his colleagues gradually came around to a conclusion that supported the view that science was a means to explore what had been created by Divine intelligence. The propagation of the human race down through the ages was very likely masterminded by a Supreme Being. The creation of the different races that comprised the human race and endowed them with the ability to reproduce had to be a well thought out process with preconditions that became part of the formula. How else could the breeding of any of these races suddenly become conditional on the proper match-up of the Z-Factor?

The recent events of the world pointed to the creative processes in the universe having entered a new phase. There was a growing sense of a powerless reaction in trying to cope with a different and yet unknown set of rules for survival. How could the White race prolong or extend its tenure on Earth? It was beginning to look like the one condition for survival was racial integration.

In addition to the ongoing tests on DNA trying to unravel the genetic code, other research activities tried to unlock the secret of conception itself. Powerful microscopes were used to observe the behavior of sperm in a laboratory dish when eggs were added and environmental conditions slightly altered. This was a repeat of the in-vitro fertilization experiment, except that in these tests, chemical additives were employed in an effort to stimulate the fertilization process. In some of the trials, even Zinc salt solutions in varying concentrations were introduced to the mixture to see if ion exchanges might result and consequently nullify the effect of the Zinc68 isotope. None of the experiments showed any degree of success. In every case, the sperm seemed to be repelled by a persistent invisible wall surrounding each female egg.

Another experiment involved a group of volunteer White married couples who were put on a controlled diet of foods rich in Zinc. The purpose for this test was to find out if massive amounts of natural Zinc ingested by the body would promote an overriding effect on the Zinc68 isotopes and thereby allow impregnation to happen. Not only were these experiments unsuccessful, but negative consequences resulted.

It had been four months since the National Laboratory for Genetics Research hosted the seminar meeting and no significant progress had been made. Tom Curtis was in his office reviewing the disappointing activities of the previous week when he got a phone call from the security officer in the lobby telling him that he had a visitor. Bob Armstrong had attended a medical meeting at the San Diego General Hospital and decided to pay Tom a surprise visit before heading back to Houston.

"Well – how does it feel to be dealing with the secrets controlling the very existence of human life?" Bob said in his jovial manner, shaking Tom's hand. He couldn't help but notice the somber expression on Tom's face. "This place never ceases to amaze me with its sophisticated equipment and clean environment; it's pervasive in the entire building complex. Can't be too many germs floating around a place like this."

"Have a seat, Bob, and make yourself at home. I hope you'll excuse my present state of mind. It's just that we are not making a lot of progress these days – and we seem to be running out of ideas."

"Look, if I caught you at a bad moment, please excuse me. I can always visit at a later time. I can appreciate how you feel – this research game can provide its share of frustrating periods. Why don't I cut this short and let you return to work?"

"Please don't do that, Bob. I need to talk to someone right now and it looks like you've been elected. Let me have my secretary, Emily, bring us a pot of coffee – then I'll bring you up-to-date on our present activities."

"I'd like that very much," Bob said. "After the discovery of the Z-Factor, you left us all in a state of anxiety about what you'd concentrate on next. You may not realize it, Tom, but you have become a famous man throughout the world – and deservedly so."

Tom waved the accolade away. "Unless we solve this riddle, it's undeserved. We've used a significant number of volunteers from all the races and the end result, in every case, comes out negative or of no significance. There is no doubt that the Z-Factor is real, but any hope of overriding its controlling grip on the human reproductive process appears impossible. Maybe the time has come to focus on getting statistics on biracial reproduction since that seems to be the way of the future.

"We have to face it sooner or later – racial integration may be our only salvation in the world to come."

"I hate to see you switch tracks after all this effort, Tom. You and your people have been circling around the problem – coming so close to a solution that could ultimately preserve the White race. It would be a shame to give up now – don't you agree?"

"I hear what you are saying, and I haven't given up just yet, but we also have to face the facts such as they might be. However – I've been thinking. We've been concentrating the bulk of our research on the White race as the problem race. We have also researched the nonwhite races on a comparative basis to establish similarities and differences with the White race.

"More recently, we have studied the prospect of integrating all the races as a solution to our survival problem. During this time, we've been so preoccupied with the actual problem of infertility within the White race that we totally neglected one small group of people who are in a class by themselves.

"It's time to test those few White couples who have borne children in the past three years. We were waiting to get to a particular knowledge base, in order to design trials that would be finely-tuned before beginning, but since we've plateaued, what are we waiting for?"

"You know something, Tom? I think you've zeroed in on a possible way to clear up this whole mess. Remember some time ago at one of our seminars, I was stressing how we should take a closer look at the unusual side of events that have taken place? What you just stated fits that approach exactly.

"That, my friend, is the essence of research. You may well have put your finger on the missing clue."

"The question is," said Tom, "how do we capture the greatest number of participants? Do we survey hospital records for White births during the past three years?

Then set up interviews in a preliminary effort to find out what is so different about these people? That kind of approach could turn out to be a pretty lengthy process. Do you know of a different way to speed it up, Bob?"

"What if you start with Ben Davidson and his wife? They're eager to help. Design a trial and use them as guinea pigs."

"Now, why didn't I think of that? They're the ideal candidates for that first interview. I'll call him up right now and find out how soon they can pay us a visit – I have his NASA phone number in our seminar directory, right here in my desk."

He placed the call to NASA, and Ben agreed to visit the National Laboratory for Genetics for a screening appointment as soon as Mary went into her ovulation phase.

"I have a plane to catch if I am to make it back to Houston tonight," Bob said, standing up to leave. He extended his arm for a parting handshake. "This was a very interesting visit, and I wish you success in the next phase of your research, Tom. Please keep us posted on new developments."

"I sure will – and thanks for dropping by, Bob." Tom's attitude bounced back to optimistic. He couldn't wait to meet with the Davidsons.

Within two weeks, Tom Curtis went out to the San Diego International Airport to pick up the Davidsons. He updated them as he drove to the Genetics Laboratory.

"Our current efforts in genetics are continuing at an accelerated pace, even though we are not progressing as fast as we'd like to. We've practically been banging our heads against the wall studying the less fortunate part of the White race and then every imaginable racial combination you could think of – without a whole lot of success."

"It's a dire situation," said Ben. "Do you realize that the world's White population has dropped by about ten percentage points in the last three years? I don't mean to interrupt your train of thought with this figure, but it certainly drives home the point of how increasingly dependent on you the entire world is becoming if this sector of humanity is to survive."

"I'm glad you appreciate the situation, Ben. That's why we're so grateful to you both for allowing us to test each of you for your Z-Factor. I'm sure it was no small feat to get someone to care for your small children for a couple days."

"The timing worked out perfectly," said Mary. "My mother was coming to visit for the month and we enlisted some extra babysitting help. And thank you so much for hosting us at your home."

"I understand what you are saying, Tom. Either of us could be the reason for our being able to have children."

"Well this is no small contribution to science you're both making. It's sincerely appreciated. We'll head first to the medical clinic to procure egg and sperm samples, then you'll do face-to-face recorded interviews with a psychologist," Tom said. "Thank you again for assisting us."

At the lab, Ben's Z-Factor proved to be as expected – Zn68 – thus proving that he was a bonafide member of the White race. The interview to establish his personal profile didn't reveal anything out of the ordinary except that he had a donor heart, but that was assumed not to be a contributing factor to his present virile condition, and they knew the donor to be White.

After the procedure to extract egg specimens from Mary, she and Ben had lunch in the cafeteria. She was scheduled for her interview with the lab's psychologist in a couple hours.

While Ben and Mary waited patiently in the conference room, Tom rushed in.

"The chemical analysis of Mary's egg specimen using the mass spectrograph came up with a surprising result: Mary's Z-Factor contained two isotopes of Zinc–ZN68 and ZN64! This must be the explanation for why you've been able to bear children. Mary, do you have an Asian branch in your genealogy?"

"No," Mary said. "I'm positive about that – my mother did a whole project researching our ancestry when she retired."

"Okay," said Tom. "I have to run to a meeting now, but I'll see you both at dinner. Molly will swing by to pick you up in about an hour.

Dr. Reilly, the psychologist has a copy of this report, so she'll ask you questions that may elicit a connection. See you both later."

Shortly, Dr. Reilly, an upbeat redhead, introduced herself and Mary's interview commenced. After her vital statistics were recorded, Dr. Reilly sought answers to the isotope mystery.

"I hope you don't take offense at this," Dr. Reilly said, "But Norwegians are known to be great seafarers and likely visited many foreign countries in their travels. Is there any chance that one of your ancestors might have brought back from his travels a new bride of Asian origin? Maybe someone that wasn't spoken about? People can be funny about that type of thing."

"No," said Mary laughing. "That's kind of far fetched if you knew my family."

"Is it possible in the generations since your relatives settled in the Minnesota area that there was a family marriage with an Asian person?"

"Not that I'm aware of."

"Can you think of any other possible contact or involvement in your family background with any individual that might have been even part Asian?"

"Believe me, Dr. Reilly, I'm not trying to hide anything from you – I have no reason to. The only contact I ever had with anyone Asian was during my early teen years when my dad was assigned to the American Embassy in Tokyo, Japan. He worked for the diplomatic service, and my family lived there for a period of four years."

"Did anything unusual or out of the ordinary happen while you lived there?"

"Not that I can think of at the moment. Actually, I have very fond memories of my time in Japan. I enjoyed my schooling, and I made lasting friendships with some of my Japanese classmates who I still correspond with.

"Oh, wait. Now that I think of it, when I was thirteen years old, I was in a car accident and my left leg was pretty badly mangled. Thanks to the wonderful care I received in the hospital, I recovered fully and don't feel any aftereffects, to this day. That's about all I can think of."

Later in the day, Tom Curtis reviewed a printed copy of Mary's personal profile and his attention was naturally drawn to the time she spent in Japan as a youngster. Right away, he suspected a connection between her bi-racial Z-Factor and her four-year stay in that country. Putting her records among his other papers in his briefcase, he'd discuss the matter further with her that evening.

During an enjoyable dinner, Tom and Ben chatted about their research programs and how they were so closely related in a common cause, in spite of their totally different scientific disciplines. Conversation about the mystery of Mary's isotope would wait for later.

After dinner, Mary helped Molly clear the dining table. Molly put up coffee, and they moved into the living room to relax.

Tom couldn't wait a minute longer before he brought up the subject of Mary's foreign travel. "Did you attend a special school for American personnel while you were there, Mary?"

"Yes, I did for the first two years. All children of the diplomatic corps along with children of military personnel attended a school run by a staff of American teachers. The school was located at one of the airbases close by.

"Then in my last year of elementary school, my parents asked me if I would like to transfer to a Japanese school so I could get more exposure to their teaching methods and their culture; so, I did. I really looked forward to learning more about them."

"Judging by your earlier comments, you made lasting friendships with some of your classmates."

"I sure did. In fact, several times during that same period, my parents let me go on weekend visits to live with the families of some of my best girlfriends."

"On a different subject, how did this accident come about that you were involved in?"

"That happened during one of my visits to the Sagura family, the parents of my good friend, Yomo. They were a middle-class family living in the suburbs of Tokyo.

"On this occasion, Mr. Sagura was driving us to the nearby mountains for a family picnic when an oncoming car wouldn't yield the right of way. He ran off the road to avoid a collision. I was thrown from the car when the door suddenly flew open, and I smashed my upper left leg against a large rock by the road."

"How badly were you hurt, Mary?" Molly asked.

"It was pretty scary. I had a deep gash about eight inches long on my thigh which was bleeding badly. I'll always be grateful to Mrs. Sagura for the way she treated me. With her nursing background, she knew exactly how to cut down the bleeding as much as possible while they rushed me to the local hospital."

"What did they do to you at the hospital?" Molly said, curious about cultural differences in the medical arena.

"Not surprisingly, I also had a broken bone in my leg which needed to be set and I had to be in a cast – but before that could be done, I needed surgery to stop the bleeding and to sew my wound shut. I must have lost a good amount of blood because they also had to give me a blood transfusion."

Both Tom and Ben suddenly leapt out of their chairs, obviously excited by Mary's account of her accident.

Ben blurted out, "Repeat what you just told us, Honey. You said you received blood plasma in a Japanese hospital?"

"That's right – I guess I never told you that part, Dear. So, I'm the one that's part Japanese!"

"That's it, Mary! There's a highly probable chance that your Z-Factor was altered by having that blood transfusion! I'd be willing to bet that you underwent a form of gene splicing and nobody even realized at the time what was happening."

At this point, everyone in the room was ecstatic over the possibility that a major breakthrough in Tom's research may have just taken place. However, he had experienced too many disappointments in recent years from experiments having high expectations and knew he'd have to get more proof.

"We should all sleep on this one – if we can – and we'll see what tomorrow brings us to support our claim. In the meantime, let's keep this quiet until we've had a chance to do a little more research – but I can't help wondering if Mary may have put us on the right track."

"At least, now you know what to look for in your hospital survey of other anomalous White couples, like Mary and myself," Ben said.

"It should be easy to accumulate statistics which will either prove or disprove what may be the solution to the salvation of the White race, "impure" as it may become, Tom said. "Why don't we all have a nightcap before retiring? In the morning, I'll take you two to the airport for your flight to San Francisco where you can start enjoying your vacation."

"I'll drink to that," said Mary, smiling.

The following morning, Molly accompanied her husband as they drove their guests to the airport. All four of them were still in a state of euphoria over their potential discovery.

Tom assured Ben and Mary that he would keep them informed promptly about the latest developments as they bid each other farewell.

After returning Molly to the condo and kissing her goodbye, Tom rushed back to the lab; he couldn't wait to tell his coworkers about the potential breakthrough.

The first item on their new agenda was to contact several of the large hospitals in the country to obtain data on White couples who had babies during the past three years. In particular, information was sought on whether one or both of the parents had been given a blood transfusion during their lifetimes. Although it would be impossible to identify the racial identity of the blood source (records only specified blood types, which were common to all races), the correlation of birth and blood transfusions, if strong enough, could help support the new theory. Where possible, the recent parents would be asked to submit to a Z-Factor test to further reinforce any correlation present.

Tom had a second item on his personal agenda because he was keyed up and anxious to see early results. He wanted to experiment with a control White group willing to undergo blood transfers from nonwhites.

As he suspected, once word got out that a new reproduction experiment was in trials, his office was swamped with volunteers – mostly childless couples eager to start families.

Since the effective amount of blood plasma to transfer was unknown, it was decided to start small and subsequently increase the dosage, in case of negative results. One hundred cc's was settled upon for the first test.

Seven couples were selected to receive blood transfusions. Out of this group, three couples were chosen for blood transfers to both husband and wife. One couple would get blood from a Black donor, another from an Asian donor; and for the third couple, one mate would get one type and the other mate, the other type. For the remaining four couples, only one mate in each pair would get a blood transfer in order to cover all combinations.

Once the transfusions had taken place, the test couples were instructed to return in one month for Z-Factor testing.

During that anxious waiting period, encouraging reports came back from hospital surveys. Out of a total of 859 White births on record from 52 hospitals, 623 of the parent couples reported one member of the two having received a blood transfusion for any one of a variety of reasons, ranging from loss of blood due to combat wounds, to accidents, to surgery. Of the remaining 236, 77 submitted to Z-Factor testing and at least one mate out of each couple proved to have dual designators. The results were assumed to be inherited traits from similar events that could have taken place in a prior generation.

The biggest surprise of all occurred at the end of the one-month waiting period. The date was November 17th, two and a half years post the cessation of White procreation.

Out of the seven test couples, four of the wives would not be able to undergo Z-Factor testing because they were pregnant. Of the remaining couples, the recipients of blood transfers all proved to have the appropriate dual designators from their lab tests. Successful impregnation of the females in those couples, bearing other fertility issues, would only be a matter of time.

THE WHITE RACE'S BIOLOGICAL CLOCK HAD BEEN RESTARTED ! ! !

When Tom Curtis reported the good news at the next review seminar, there was a wild outburst of jubilation as the scientific community of the entire world finally reaped the reward for its super-human efforts in pursuing the answer to the most formidable riddle of all time.

32

When the news was released to the press that the White race would once again be able to procreate after a forty-six month hiatus, there was widespread pandemonium throughout the world. All races on Earth now shared a common bond and were united in a joint effort for survival. Racial prejudice was vanquished as there was no longer an "us" and "them." Humanity was expected to live out its time on the planet for as long as Nature allowed it.

Blood transfusions were made available to couples around the world so that everyone could reproduce. The procedure was reminiscent of the ancient Native American ritual intended to create "blood brothers" through the exchange of blood via self-inflicted wounds – a token gesture of lasting friendship with their White brothers. The chemistry inherent in blood sharing turned out to be the salvation of the White race. Well, the seemingly "White" race.

The salvation of the White race had been allowed by Nature as if it was meant to be, but only after every race inhabiting the Earth came to realize their common bond as products of the Creation. The merging of the White race with all other host races would occur during the present generation. In future times, the White race would never be quite the same.

On a more somber note – what should be done about bringing to justice the mad terrorists who had brutally killed so many white people during their insane quest to wipe out the entire race? The task of hunting them down is in the hands of the FBI, Scotland Yard, and INTERPOL.

The time had come to unify all races on earth during their wait for nature's next move.

EPILOGUE

So much for fiction—and now—back to reality. Humans, like all other creatures that have inhabited the planet Earth, are quite fragile. We are prone to make errors in judgment where the wellbeing of our fellowman may be at stake. The proverbial fork in the road often calls upon us to make decisions which could be disastrous to humankind on our one and only planet. Too often in our society, important decisions by individuals have been self-serving without due regard to possible consequences.

Actually, Nature has always been in charge and the best that we can do is try to adapt to its changing ways. Fortunately for the human race – thus far – good has triumphed over evil. However, it is yet to be seen whether permanent consequences, due to greed, will arise that the world will be helpless to overcome. We currently have the ability to destroy life on our singularly life-sustaining planet— at a moment's notice.

Let us never forget that the vast expanse of the universe is Nature's arena; humankind has merely a bit part in that colossal tale of TIME. For all we know, the universe will remain a paradox for eons to come.

The story you just read could well have signaled The End of the Beginning of creation, which took some 18 or so billion years to manifest. Perhaps the next phase in TIME will be the collapse of the universe on itself, lasting for another 18 or so billion years. Today could herald the onset of The Beginning of the End. So —in OUR long term — humanity, if it wisely takes care of itself, could remain in existence far into the unforeseeable future.

ABOUT THE AUTHOR

Louis Daigle was born in VanBuren, Maine during the depression years. As a young man in the forties when WWII broke out, he enlisted in the Army Air Corps and became an aerial navigator on a B-29 heavy bomber.

The war's end led Daigle to the University of Maine where he earned a degree in Engineering Physics. Soon after graduation he joined the U.S. Naval Research Lab in Washington D.C.

Following that, the majority of Lou's career was spent working for a New York based aircraft manufacturing company and a Connecticut aerospace firm.

Lou retired in 1987 and set to work writing *Time Window*.

Today at age 91, Lou resides in Wakefield Rhode Island with his wife Terry of 66 years, the childhood sweetheart with whom he has spent his life.

www.ingramcontent.com/pod-product-compliance
Lightning Source LLC
Chambersburg PA
CBHW070923180626
46817CB00003B/1175